Bean Wishing for a Latte Love

Tia Marlee

A Novel Choice Press

Book Cover by Beck and Dot

Editing by Lia Huntington

This book is dedicated to my grandmother who always had a cup of coffee in her hand.

Contents

Chapter One

Knox

GOLDFISH CRACKERS CRUNCH UNDER the weight of my knee pushing down on the fancy three-hundred-dollar car seat I've installed for Matthias. I sigh. My once-pristine Lincoln SUV is now a graveyard for fish crumbs. As a thirty-year-old bachelor, this is not how I saw my life going. I brush the crumbs out of the car seat, making a mental note to vacuum on my next day off.

Yeah, right. Days off aren't free time. Not anymore. When my sister told me being a parent was a full-time job, I should have listened. I laughed when she tried to tell me how different life with a child would be. I brushed her off. What were the odds I'd ever have to step into *that* role? I glance at the toddler in my arms. Higher than I thought, apparently.

Clearing my throat, I settle Matthias into his seat and brush the hair from his forehead, ignoring the bright green marker on his cheeks. Light brown locks, just like his mom. His watery blue eyes, still swollen from crying, were from his dad. I pinch the bridge of my nose to keep the emotions at bay. Definitely don't have time to fall apart this morning. Matti won the coin toss for breakdowns this morning. I didn't realize such a small kid could make such a big noise.

Apparently telling him markers weren't makeup wasn't the way to go. I grab my ear lobe and give it a tug. My ears are still ringing.

Though, to be fair, I almost joined him when the coffee machine decided to spit out wet grounds instead of the glorious nectar of the morning I'd been counting on. Now, I barely have time to drop him off at Mrs. Wilson's and grab a coffee on the way to work.

I sigh again, thinking about the high-end machine that is now a counter ornament. At least until I figure out why it's not working. That hurts. I'm pretty sure I'm seventy-five percent coffee, and twenty-five percent self doubt these days.

Checking that Matti is securely buckled, I grin. It only took two YouTube videos and a call to the local fire station to convince me I've installed the seat correctly.

Matti turns his deep blue eyes in my direction and frowns. "Mamaaa," he whines.

"I know, buddy. I'm sorry." Climbing into the car, I shut the door and rest my head on the steering wheel. Tears prick the backs of my eyes. Explaining to a three-year-old his mom and dad are gone forever, and he's stuck with his uncle, hasn't been easy. The pediatrician keeps telling me to give him more time.

Matti lays his head against the seat and looks out the window. I don't know how to comfort him, and it kills me. "You're going to Mrs. Wilson's today," I say, as I back out of the driveway and make a right. I'm hoping seeing Mrs. Wilson will cheer him up. I roll the windows down, letting the cool breeze soothe us both.

The drive passes in relative silence, and fifteen minutes later, I pull into Mrs. Wilson's driveway. I get out of the car and open Matti's door to unbuckle him when I notice he doesn't have his shoes on anymore. "Hey Matti, where are your shoes?" I ask, looking around the floorboard and seat around him. He shrugs and kicks his legs. I unbuckle him and take him out of the car seat, hoping they're behind him. No such luck.

"Matti," I ask, trying not to panic. "Where are your shoes?"

Matti giggles and points to the road. "Outside."

I walk to the edge of the driveway and look down the road as far as I can see in both directions. No shoes.

"Matti, did you throw your shoes out the window?" I call loudly enough he can hear me in the car.

Matti laughs and kicks his feet. "Bye bye."

"Matti, it's January. It's too cold for you to not have shoes on," I say. *What was he thinking?*

Just then, Mrs. Wilson's door swings open. "Knox, what are you doing standing by the road?"

"I ..." I suck in a breath as I think of a way to word this without swearing. "Matti seems to think it's funny to toss his shoes out the car window while we are driving," I say, exasperation filling my voice. I walk back to the car and lift Matti from the car seat.

Mrs. Wilson laughs and holds her hands out to the toddler. "You left his window down the entire way here?"

I nod. "I was hoping the cool air would give us both a reset for the day."

She frowns. "What happened? Why does Matthias look like the Grinch?"

"He found the markers while I was making him breakfast. By the way, he doesn't like eggs anymore, apparently. He liked eggs yesterday, but today, no eggs."

She laughs. "Toddlers change their minds like that. It's normal."

I run my hands through my hair. "If you say so," I grumble. "How am I supposed to know what to feed him if he keeps changing his mind overnight? I think the grocery store has increased its profits by at least fifty percent since I moved here."

Mrs. Wilson lets out a loud laugh. "You'll figure it out," she says, patting me on the arm. "Ready to go inside, Matti?"

Matti nods and pulls at her graying hair, before laying his head on her shoulder. "You get going so you won't be late. When you pick Matti up tonight, I need to talk to you about something."

A feeling of dread sparks in the pit of my stomach. "Okay," I say, reaching out and patting Matti on the back. He gives me a smile and a wave. I shake my head and wonder if I'll ever be able to understand toddlers like Mrs. Wilson can. "Thanks for helping, Mrs. Wilson."

She waves me off with a flick of her wrist and heads back up the driveway and into the house. I take one last look at the empty road and sigh. She's right. If I don't get a move on, I'm going to be late.

I'm grateful that Mrs. Wilson agreed to keep watching Matthias after the court awarded me custody of him. Though, in the beginning, her sour attitude made me wonder if she disagreed with Sarah and Les's decision to name me guardian.

It probably doesn't help that on my first night alone with him, I called her in a panic. He'd created his own art project in his crib, and I did not know what I was doing. Thankfully, a few heavy sighs and simple instructions got everyone and everything cleaned up in no time.

I glance at the time on my dash and frown. Fingers crossed the little coffee shop I've noticed near work isn't too busy this early.

Pulling into a space in front of the Coffee Loft, I peek inside. There's a line, of course, but it seems to be moving quickly.

I'll take my chances.

Once in line, I glance around the space. Bright windows let in the morning light, making the room feel welcoming. Small tables take up most of the dining area, save one cushy booth in the back. Weird. At least it smells good in here—like coffee and sugar, the best morning combination.

A chalkboard menu hangs above the counter. Several special seasonal flavors are listed—gingerbread latte, eggnog latte, winter spiced coffee, peppermint hot cocoa—as well as a small assortment of breakfast items. My stomach growls, reminding me that although I fed Matti, I failed to eat this morning.

When it's my turn, I step up to the counter, still reading the menu board. "I'll take a large regular hot coffee, cream and sugar, and a blue donut." My mouth drops open. The barista has blue hair. *Blue.* I give myself a mental shake as a knowing grin splits her face. "I'm sorry. I mean, a glazed donut. Please? Your hair is lovely, er ..."

The barista chuckles. "Can I get a name for your order?"

"Knox."

"Okay, Knox. Coming right up." She presses some buttons on the computer and calls out my order to the young woman currently filling cups at the other end of the counter. "That'll be eight dollars and fifty-three cents."

I dig out my wallet and place a ten-dollar bill on the counter. "Keep the change." I step back and wait for my name to be called. My eyes slide to the blue-haired beauty currently helping the next customer. She really is stunning. I wonder what she'd look like with her natural hair color, which I'm guessing is brown, judging by her eyebrows. Do people dye their eyebrows?

"Knox, your order's ready."

Realizing I've been staring, I quickly grab my steaming coffee and donut from the pickup counter. Spinning on my heel, I slam right into a table. In the process, I squeeze the coffee cup too tight, causing the lid to pop off and hot liquid to splash all over me. In a panic, I drop the cup, and the remaining coffee spills out, leaving a colossal mess spread across what seems like the entire floor, even though it's probably only about six feet in all directions.

I groan as I feel the warm coffee soak through my clothes.

This day is off to a great start.

Chapter Two

Lacey

THE CLANG OF METAL chairs crashing onto the tile floor causes everyone to pause. Knox Sullivan looks down at the coffee soaking his scrubs and spreading out around his feet. He mumbles something colorful under his breath.

"I'll be right back," I say to the woman who is next in line.

I grab the mop and bucket from the back and rush around the counter. Ashlan, my friend and co-worker, and Knox are already doing their best to sop up the hot liquid. "Ash, can you grab the 'wet floor' sign, please?"

She nods and springs up from her crouched position beside the handsome—if frazzled—Knox Sullivan.

"I'm so sorry," he says, wiping sticky hands on his deep blue scrubs.

"No worries." I wipe the mop over the spill and soak up most of the mess. "It happens more often than you'd think." I try not to notice the way the spilled coffee has turned his scrubs into a wetsuit. Nope, I don't notice that he has a washboard stomach. Not at all.

How much coffee fits in these cups, anyway?

Ashlan places the wet floor sign in front of the spill and nods. "It really does. At least twice a week."

Knox sighs. "That really doesn't make me feel much better." He shoots a glance to the line of people waiting for their morning fix. "Sorry," he says to them.

Ashlan slips behind the counter and washes her hands before making him another cup. "Here you go," she says, handing the steaming coffee to him. "I hope your day gets better." She flashes a grin and goes back to work taking orders and making coffee while I finish cleaning up the mess.

"Can I help?" Knox asks, pointing to the mop.

"Nope." I wring out the dirty mop and swipe it across the mess one last time. "I've got it."

He holds up the fresh coffee and the bag he'd managed not to drop. "Thanks. I'm sorry to be so much trouble."

I laugh. "Really, it's fine. You should go. You're probably late."

His eyes go wide, as if he's just realized that time has continued marching forward. "Thanks. See you," he says before heading toward the door, a bit more cautiously this time.

🌠 🌠 🌠 🌠 🌠

Finally, the morning rush is over. Ashlan and I are doing our midday clean and restock when the door swings open.

"Hey, Lacey," my friend Samantha says, shaking out her umbrella. "The sky just opened up and dumped out every bucket in the shed. I hope it doesn't ice."

"It's January in Arkansas. Anything can happen." I peer outside. "It's really coming down, though." Thank goodness we have a huge mat at the front door for days like this. Still, I grab the wet floor sign that's leaning against the end of the counter from the spill this morning, and pop it open near the entrance.

"What can I get you?" Ashlan asks, taking over behind the counter.

Samantha takes her time looking at the menu. "How about a lofty-sized caramel apple macchiato?"

"You got it." Ashlan rings her up and then moves to the other end of the counter to make her coffee.

I finish wiping the coffee rings from the tables—souvenirs from this morning's rush—and slip back behind the counter. I drop the dirty rag in the laundry bucket and wash my hands. "What brings you out in the middle of the day?"

Samantha grabs her coffee from the counter and sits at the nearest table. "I was hoping to talk to you, actually."

"Oh?"

Samantha takes a sip of the steaming hot coffee and lets out a contented sigh. "Coffee always makes things better, don't you think?"

I laugh. "I wouldn't be working at a coffee shop if I didn't think so."

She nods. "True. Do you have a minute to sit?"

I glance around the empty space and nod. "Sure. What did you want to talk about?" I ask, sliding into the vacant seat across from her.

"Well, the library has a toddler story-and-craft time. We have a volunteer who runs it, but she's having surgery and will be out for the next two weeks." She pauses and takes another sip of her coffee. "Anyway, we can't cancel it. We've had a ton of families sign up through our website."

"I'm sorry to hear that," I say, wondering what any of that has to do with me.

"I know it's not your own hands-on learning center, but would you consider filling in for story-and-craft time?" Samantha smiles at me. "Please?"

"What would that entail? Reading aloud and leading a craft?" I ask, not sold. My dream is to have a center with art, music, and science presented as play. My degree is in early childhood education, for goodness' sake. Not arts and crafts.

"Well, in part," Samantha says. "But I'd really love it if I could pass this off to you entirely. The planning ... everything. The woman, Nancy, who's been running it has some lesson plans if you'd like to follow those, or you could come up with your own."

I sit back in the chair, my mind working through what she's saying.

"I know it's not exactly what you dreamed about when you came back to Piney Brook, but it would really help me out. Plus, you may get some families who would be interested in your program. Who knows, maybe you'll meet someone with expendable cash who would be interested in investing in the center. Though I still don't know why you won't let Bryce help you."

"You know why," I say, a bit more sternly than I'd intended. I soften my tone and try again. "Bryce is living his dream, and he got there on his own. I want to do the same. Besides, I don't want to owe my brother a bunch of money if things don't work out the way I hope they will."

Samantha and I have been friends since grade school. That's the joys of growing up in a town small enough to only have one elementary school and one class per grade—you got to know everyone you went to school with. I seriously doubt I'll magically meet an investor, but she's right—it would be good to get to know some of the kids and parents better.

"I don't know. Would I be able to switch up the activities? Include some hands-on science or music and art?" My mind is already spinning with ideas. I may only have two weeks, but this could be my chance to show the parents of Piney Brook a sampling of what I hope to offer.

"Of course. This would be your project for the next few weeks. But," she says, pausing. "I can't afford to pay you. It's a volunteer position."

I nod my head. "Who will pay for the supplies?"

Samantha takes a sip of her coffee and moans a bit. "This is seriously so good. I love when you guys have the special flavors!" She sets the coffee down in front of her and picks up a napkin, dabbing at the corners of her mouth. "The library has a budget for supplies, so that shouldn't be a problem as long as we keep it pretty simple."

I sit back in my chair to think. Am I really considering this? Excitement sparks in my chest.

I am.

"What day is it scheduled for?"

Samantha grins. "Thursday mornings at ten."

"I am free on Thursdays," I say. "Can I get back to you?"

"That's fine. The sooner you let me know, the better. If you can't take it on, I'm not sure what I'll do."

I nod my head. "I'll think about it."

Samantha beams at me and claps her hands together. "Thank you so much! You're saving my behind."

"I didn't say yes yet." I laugh. "I don't know about saving anything, but it sounds like a fun opportunity."

The door chimes when a new customer walks in. I stand and push my seat back in.

"Thanks for talking with me," Samantha says, gathering her things. "I better get back to the library, and it looks like you need to get back to work."

I wave goodbye as Samantha steps back outside, opening her umbrella against the rain.

"Welcome to the Coffee Loft. What can I get you?"

"I'll take a small peppermint hot cocoa, please." The woman, dressed in scrubs, points to the pastry case. "And a cinnamon roll, too."

"You got it," I say. I ring her up and make her coffee while Ashlan puts her cinnamon roll on a plate.

"Here you go," I say, sliding the tray towards her. "Are you just getting off or going in?"

"Just going in," she says.

"I hope you have a great night," I say, smiling. She smiles back and takes her tray to a table by the windows. I wonder how Knox Sullivan's day has gone.

Chapter Three

Knox

THANK GOODNESS I KEEP a spare set of scrubs in my locker at work. I've smelled like a coffee shop all day, but at least my clothes aren't sticking to me. Several patients wrinkled their noses during my examinations. I'd laugh if I weren't also getting sick of smelling myself. Two ambulances pulled up from an accident just as I got here this morning, which took precedence over a shower—I was lucky I got to change. Day's almost over now, though.

"Hey, doc," Briella, my assigned nurse, says, grinning. "You made it." She points to her watch.

I glance around, noticing the night-shift ER doctor is already milling about. Weekdays are usually less busy, but today has been nonstop. I'm exhausted. "Thanks Briella."

After checking in with the next shift, I head to the locker room to pick up my coffee-covered scrubs. I'll have to remember to bring in an extra set when I come in for my next shift. Making sure I have all my things, I close my locker and head to the car.

As soon as I step through the sliding glass doors of the hospital, I inhale deeply. Fresh air. I will say one good thing about living in a small-town away from the hustle and bustle of a city is that the air always smells clean.

Ducking out from the overhang at the entrance, I put my coffee covered clothes over my head and trot to the car. Of course it's raining.

I get in the SUV and throw my wet and probably stained clothes into the trunk as far away from my nose as I can get them. I turn the car on and start the wipers. I'll have to carry Matti to the car when I pick him up from Mrs. Wilsons. I shake my head. I still can't believe he tossed his shoes out the window.

I've been able to put off thinking about Mrs. Wilson and whatever she needed to talk about, but now that my shift is over, it's at the forefront of my mind. I don't know what I'd do without her. My hours don't always align with daycare, and I wouldn't know where to find a nanny.

Pulling into Mrs. Wilson's driveway, I sigh. Whatever it is, I'll deal with it. I knock on the door and wait.

"Come in," Mrs. Wilson says, opening her door. "What's that smell?" she asks, wrinkling her nose.

"I spilled my coffee this morning," I say as I step inside and slide off my shoes. "How did it go today?" I ask, looking around for Matti.

"Did you swim in it?" she asks, laughing. "Today was just fine," she says, pointing to the living room. "Have a seat on the couch. Matti's just finishing a snack in the kitchen."

Without a backward glance, she walks past me toward the rear of her house where the kitchen is. I step into the living room and glance around. Pictures take up every available surface. Her children and grandchildren, I assume. I feel a bit guilty knowing that Mrs. Wilson missed out on the holidays with her family because she stayed here to help me with Matti. Doctors don't get holidays off.

Stepping over the toys on the ground, I head toward the dated-looking sofa and sit down. It's probably as old as I am, but it's comfortable. I rub my feet across the shag carpeting while I wait for Mrs. Wilson to come back. I've not seen this color in a home before—some kind of burnt orange swirl I think went out of style in the eighties. The sound of little footsteps slapping against the tile of the hallway makes me smile.

Matti.

He runs into the living room and stops.

"Hey, buddy, did you have a good day?"

He nods. I put my arms out for a hug, and he barrels into me. I close my eyes. These are the moments that give me hope.

"Knox," Mrs. Wilson's voice cuts through my thoughts. "I know that you've been settling in with Matti, and it looks like he's getting more used to you." She raises a brow and nods her head in the direction of Matti, who's now sitting beside me on the couch running a toy car up and down his legs.

"I think we are moving in the right direction," I say, trying not to be defensive. I know she means well, and really, she's helped me so much with Matti that I don't have it in me to be anything but grateful. Even if sometimes her advice comes off a bit more matter-of-fact than I'd like.

She nods. "I agree. That's why I feel comfortable with my decision."

It feels as if someone is gripping my heart in a vise. "Your decision?"

"To move." She's all smiles, as if she'd just shared the best news ever.

Could this day get any worse?

I stare at her, dumbfounded. "Move? Where?" Panic makes my palms sweat, but I can't lose my cool. Matti depends on me to stay calm. Besides, it's Mrs. Wilson. She's been a staple in this community for years from what I hear. I doubt she's moving far. *Please don't be moving far!*

"To Colorado. My daughter is having another baby, and I want to be closer."

I close my eyes. I can't fault her for wanting to be closer to her daughter and grandchildren, but Colorado? That may as well be a different country.

"Don't look like that," she says sternly. "You'll be fine."

I open my eyes and shake my head. "When do you leave?"

She grimaces. "Two weeks. I had planned to move two months ago, but ..." she trails off.

Two weeks? *Two weeks?* I take a deep breath. "We're going to miss you, but I understand. Thanks for letting me know."

"For what it's worth," she says, taking a seat next to Matti. "I think you're doing a great job with him."

I glance at the little boy sitting beside me. "Even though he chucked his shoes out the window this morning?" I ask sarcastically.

She grins. "Knox, every parent goes through things like missing shoes and crib surprises. It doesn't mean you're doing anything wrong."

I sigh. "Thanks."

"I wouldn't be moving if I didn't think you two were going to be okay," she says, reaching over Matti and patting my hand.

* * * * *

Matti's giggles are the first thing I hear the next morning. I groan and look at the clock on the nightstand. Six a.m.? Who knew little kids were such early risers? I kick the covers off and swing my legs over the side of the bed. Stretching my arms above my head, I vow to have a better day than yesterday. As if I have control over anything these days.

I step into Matti's room and smile. The curly-headed boy is standing in his crib, though from the looks of it, we'll need to upgrade soon. The pale blue walls are accented with decals of bats, baseballs, bases, and players. There's even a framed, signed jersey on the wall above the crib—number thirty-seven, Eli Weaver, left fielder for the Ozarks Legends. A nod to his dad's obsession with the local team.

It's been strange living in my sister's house the past few months, but I didn't want to uproot Matthias from the only home he's ever known, too. It was a simple decision to move to Piney Brook. My sister always talked about how much she loved this small-town, and since I've moved here, I can see why.

"Good Morning," I say, lifting Matthias from the crib and tucking him into my side. "Sleep well?"

Matti touches my face and smiles. "I hungy."

Ever since the accident, Matti's language has regressed. For a while, he hardly spoke at all. He's talking more now, but I can't help but worry about him. The pediatrician said it should come back to normal as time goes on. Still, I make a mental note to look up speech therapists in the area.

"Let's get you cleaned up, and then we will go out for breakfast." Unless, by some miracle, the coffee machine decides to work this morning, we will need to venture out and get some.

By the time I get us both ready and pack an extra pair of shoes, just in case, it's already after seven. The drive to the Coffee Loft is short, thankfully. I open Matti's door to lift him out of the car seat, and see that his shoes are gone again.

I learned my lesson though, and left the window up, so I find them on the other side of the back seat.

"Matti. You have to keep your shoes on when we go places," I remind him. "It's cold outside. We don't want your toes to freeze and fall off."

He just kicks his feet in response. I chuckle. I wish I could be so carefree.

Once he's dressed again, I balance him on my hip and set off in the direction of the coffee shop. The smell of freshly brewed goodness greets me as I swing open the door. The same blue-haired barista is working today, and for some reason I don't want to think about too much, it brings a smile to my face.

"I hungy!" Matti shouts, wiggling to be let down.

"Well, let's order. Do you want a scone and chocolate milk?" I ask having scanned the menu for kid friendly options first.

"Yes," he says, still squirming. "I get down now."

"Okay, but hold my hand. I don't want you to get hurt." I set Matti down on his feet and take his hand. "Let's get in line so we can order."

When it's our turn, I hold Matti up so he can see the pastries in the case near the register. "Which one do you want?"

He points to a blueberry scone. "Dat one."

"Hi, again." The beautiful barista with the colorful hair greets us with a smile.

I glance at the name on her Coffee Loft apron. *Lacey—that's right.* "Hi."

"What can I get for you two this morning?"

"We'll take two blueberry scones, a chocolate milk, and a lofty coffee with cream and sugar, please."

She nods and rings in the order. I give Matti the credit card to hand her, and he immediately throws it behind the counter.

"Matti," I groan. "You were supposed to hand it to her, not throw it."

Lacey laughs, a full-on belly laugh. It's cute.

"It's fine," she says, still laughing a bit. "Happens ..."

"More often than I'd think?" I finish.

She nods. "Yeah."

She runs the card and hands it back. "Why don't you find a table, and we'll bring your order out to you. Looks like your hands are full this morning, Dad."

I hesitate and wonder if I should correct her, but there's a line forming behind me, so I decide to let it go. Besides, I'm the closest thing the kid's got now, and Matti is so busy squirming to get down that he didn't seem to notice.

I set Matti back on the ground, and tell him to pick us a table. He pulls me to the back corner to the cozy booth that looks more like a rounded sofa than a table. "Here," he says, jumping up onto the bench and wiggling toward the middle.

"Here looks great," I say, sliding in beside him.

Chapter Four

Lacey

I WOULDN'T HAVE GUESSED Knox had a son. I glance over to where they're both sitting in the booth, fidgeting. Like father, like son, I suppose.

I place their order on a tray and take it to their table. "Here we are," I say, setting the coffee out of the way from the reach of small hands. "And here's yours, sir," I say with a bow to the little boy. He grins and takes his milk. Setting the scones on the table, I smile at Knox. "Anything else I can get you, Knox?"

He looks startled for a moment. "You remember my name?"

I laugh. "Well, it's unique. Plus, you paid with a card, so it was easy to figure out."

"Oh, yeah," he says.

"Anything else I can get you?" I ask again.

"Not unless you know someone who has experience with children and would like a job," he says, chuckling a bit.

"Oh," I say, surprised. "What kind of job?"

He takes a sip of the hot coffee and sighs. I don't know why that's the reaction everyone has to a first sip of coffee. It's like when you see a cute baby and smile. It's just what's done.

"Well, I just found out my nanny is moving to Colorado," he says. "I have two weeks to find a replacement."

"Oh." I nod. "Mrs. Wilson?"

He looks up at me. "How did you know?"

She laughs. "It's a small-town. Not much stays private in a small-town. Although, I didn't know the new doctor had a son. So, you managed to keep that one a secret." I wink at him. Then blink rapidly. *What in the world? You don't wink at customers, Lacey.*

"Do you have something in your eye?" Knox asks, pushing up to stand. "Where's your sink? We should flush it out."

A high-pitched chortle reaches my ears, and I'm stunned when I realize it came from me. "No, I'm fine. It's out already. An eyelash or something."

"Are you sure?" He stands there, bent down over me, looking into my eyes as though he can see the offending item sticking to my eyeball.

"Yeah," I squeak. "So, about this job," I say, trying to change the subject. "What are you looking for—in case I know someone?" I love my job at the Coffee Loft, but if I want to open my own center one day, I'll need more than my barista salary to do it.

"Well, my hours at the hospital are long. I usually work three twelve-hour shifts one week, and four the next. I'm always off on Wednesdays and Saturdays. Most of my shifts are days. I had it worked into my contract. Though occasionally, I run late due to an emergency."

I nod. "What are you thinking in terms of pay?"

He pauses and takes a bite of scone. Checking on the little boy who is currently breaking his scone into a crumbly mess on the table instead of eating it. "Matti, are you eating or playing?" he asks.

"Playing," Matti says, grinning and going back to his task. Knox sighs.

"Well, I was thinking around thirty dollars an hour to start." He glances at the mess Matti is making and shakes his head. "But I don't know what's fair. I'm still new to this parenting gig."

I raise a brow, but keep my questions to myself. I glance at his hand. No ring. I wonder where Matti's mom is.

He must notice, because he grins at me for a second. "I'm Matti's uncle. My sister, Sarah, and her husband, Les, were in an accident a few months ago."

I gasp. "Oh. Oh, my. I'm so sorry." Of course I knew about the accident. It made the front page of the newspaper. I'd never met the couple, but those who had said they'd been wonderful people.

"Thanks," he says, looking down at his scone.

"Play now?" Matti asks, bouncing in the seat.

"I'll let you finish your breakfast," I say, stepping away from the table.

He nods and pops the last third of the scone into his mouth.

"Park?" Matti asks again.

I glance behind me in time to see Knox nod. He stands and walks to the counter where I'm wiping the same spot over and over again, trying not to stare openly. He pulls out his wallet, and hands me a business card. "That's my cell phone number. If you know of anyone who might be interested in watching this little guy, please let me know."

I nod and take the card, sliding it into my pocket. "Will do," I say, trying to figure out how I could work at the Coffee Loft and nanny. Thirty dollars an hour is more than I make now. If I could do both, I'd have the money I need to start my business sooner rather than later.

The moment Knox leaves, Ashlan is squealing. "Did I hear that correctly? He's looking for a nanny and paying almost double what you make here?"

I nod my head. "Yeah, but I have a job." I pick up a towel and wipe down the parts of the countertop I'd missed while gawking at the handsome doctor. "Besides, Samantha just asked me to take on the children's programming at the library for a few weeks."

Ashlan smiles. "Who says you can't do both?"

"Me," I state flatly. "How would I be able to work here, nanny, and pull off the children's program?"

She laughs. "How did you work full time and go to school full time? You schedule, you plan."

"I'm sure there's someone else out there who would be a great nanny."

"Not as great as you, and you know it. You've always loved kids. You have a heart for this kind of thing. I don't know why you aren't turning in your notice here, like—right now, and taking that fine man up on his offer."

I gasp. "Ashlan! I love my job here. Are you trying to get rid of me?"

She laughs. "Not at all. I just know when a wonderful opportunity shows itself."

"I'll think about it," I say.

✿ ✿ ✿ ✿ ✿

After work, I decide to grab some food from Beats and Eats. Gabby is working tonight, and I could use a friendly ear.

"Hey there," Gabby says as she reaches the hostess stand. "What are you doing here this afternoon?"

I shrug. "I was hungry?"

She laughs. "Are you asking me, or telling me?"

"Both." I sigh. "It's been a weird few days. What time are you off today?"

Gabby looks at the large clock above the kitchen. "I get off in about an hour. Want to grab something to eat and wait?"

I nod. "That would be great."

She leads me to a table near the counter, but far enough away from others that they won't overhear if we chat a bit.

"Thanks," I say, sliding into the booth.

"Girl, I got you. Anytime." She hands me a menu and says she'll be right back with a Diet Coke. I don't know what I'd do without her. She's been my friend since second grade when T.J. knocked my pencil case on the floor and stepped on my favorite pencil, snapping it in half. I cried. I couldn't help it. Gabby came to my rescue, calling him a meanie head and giving me her favorite pencil to use.

"So," she says, setting the cold drink on the table. "What can I get you?"

"The usual," I say, handing her back the menu without even looking at it.

She rolls her eyes. "You don't want to try anything new?"

I shake my head. "I know what I like."

"Alrighty then, a chicken strip salad with ranch dressing and extra cheese. Coming right up." She shakes her head as she walks away to put in my order.

I take a drink of the cold soda and look around the space. The same faces I've seen my whole life. It's comforting, but sometimes I wish something exciting would happen to me. My mind goes back to Knox and Matti. Could I take on the nanny position?

Determined to put the decision out of my mind for a while, I take out my Kindle and open up the latest rom-com I downloaded. I'm just getting into the story when Ms. Daisy, the owner of Beats and Eats, drops my salad off at my table.

"Here you go," she says. "I put an extra ranch on the side for you. Just in case." She winks and walks over to a table that has caught her attention.

Ms. Daisy groans about being ready to retire, but I think she secretly enjoys keeping up with everyone in town when they come in.

I take a bite of my salad and let myself get lost in the book while I eat.

"So, what's up, buttercup?" Gabby asks, sliding into the chair across from me.

Startled, I look up from my Kindle. "You're done already?"

Gabby chuckles. "Good book?"

I nod, flipping the cover closed and sliding the Kindle back into my purse. "It really is."

She eyes me skeptically. "If you say so," she says.

"I do," I say, putting a hand over my heart. "Swoony book boyfriends never break your heart!"

She raises a brow. "I'll take fantasy books over romance any day."

"You don't know what you're missing," I say, cringing after the words leave my mouth. Gabby used to enjoy a good romance book, but stopped reading them shortly after her friend Heath left for his first deployment. "I just mean, in the books, the girl gets the guy and there's always a happily ever after. Unlike real life." I roll my eyes.

"Yeah, in real life the girl doesn't always get the guy," she says sadly. "Anyway, what did you want to do?"

"Want to walk around the square and window shop while we talk?" I love the town square. Every Christmas, it's decorated to the nines with a tree lighting ceremony and vendors. "We can see what they're doing with their window displays now that the holidays are over."

"Sure, just let me grab my purse." She stands and heads into the back of the restaurant.

I slip my bag over my shoulder and stand, stretching my back. "Ready?" I ask when she returns.

"Yep."

We walk toward the front door. I push the door open for her to go through, and it smacks right into someone. "Oh, I'm so ..." Flames lick up my neck and heat my cheeks. "Knox. I'm so sorry," I say. "Where's Matti?"

"It's no problem," he says, grinning. "Fancy *bumping* into you here." He snorts. "Get it?"

I laugh, his excitement over his joke too hard to resist. "I do."

"Are you going to introduce us?" Gabby asks, stepping around me and out the door.

Chapter Five

Knox

"Of course," Lacey says, brushing her blue hair out of her face. "Gabby, this is Knox. Knox, my best friend, Gabby."

"Nice to meet you," I say, shaking Gabby's hand. "Matti is with Mrs. Wilson," I say, answering Lacey's earlier question. "I had an appointment this afternoon, so she's watching him."

She nods and glances at Gabby.

"Have you thought of anyone who might be up for the nanny position?" I ask hopefully.

"A nanny position?" Gabby asks, looking from me to Lacey.

"Yeah," Lacey says. "Knox is a doctor at the hospital. He's looking for someone to watch his nephew while he works."

Gabby claps her hands together. "You should do it," she says, grinning. "You're great with kids."

"I have a job, remember?" Lacey looks at Gabby, sending her some sort of secret message.

How do women do that?

"Well, yeah, but it's part-time. Weren't you just saying you were trying to find a second job to save up for the center?"

My head bounces back and forth between them as they volley back and forth. It's exhausting, like watching the fuzzy yellow ball at a tennis match. "Wait," I say, my brain finally catching up. "What center?"

"Lacey has a degree in early childhood education. She wants to open an enrichment center for young kids to experience art, science, and music with kid-friendly, hands-on activities," Gabby says, throwing an arm around Lacey and squeezing.

"Not *just* those things. But yes. In a nutshell, that's what I want to do. One day."

"That's amazing," I say, really taking in the blue-haired beauty in front of me. I'd assumed she didn't have serious life goals. It's not fair of me, but I'd judged her on her hair and her job.

I should know better.

Lacey shrugs. "It would be, if I could save up enough to get started."

"I have an idea," I drawl. "What days do you work at the Coffee Loft?"

She looks at me, her brows drawn together in confusion. "Usually Monday, Wednesday, and Saturday."

"So the only day that overlaps is Monday. I wonder if I could find someone else for that day." Knox tips his head to the side, his brows drawn together as he thinks.

"Or," Gabby starts. "You could drop down to two days a week at the Coffee Loft."

Lacey looks at her curiously. "I could always see if that is an option."

"Would you be okay with that?" I ask. "I don't want to interfere with your life too much." Though I would like to help her with her goals. It could be a win-win situation. My insides tremble in anticipation. When's the last time I felt this spark of excitement?

It's been a while. Before the accident. If I'm being honest, I haven't felt so strongly about something since I decided to go into emergency medicine.

She takes her time, thinking it over. "I work early those days. How late would you be getting home?"

"I'm usually home by seven-thirty." Excitement builds in my gut. This could be amazing. Lacey has the credentials, and she obviously cares about children if she wants to open an enrichment center one day. The way I feel has absolutely nothing to do with how her eyes sparkle when we are standing this close. Or how her smile makes her shine like the sun.

"That's not too late," she says. "I guess I could talk to Aurora and Ashlan. See if I could drop my Monday shift. Now that the holidays are over, it might work."

"That would be great. I'd pay you more if it helps." I'm desperate, and I could afford to pay a little more to make sure that Matthias is in expert hands while I work.

She laughs. "I don't need you to pay me more. I just need to figure out if I can juggle everything."

"What else do you have going on?" Gabby asks.

"I told Samantha I'd run the story time at the library starting next week."

Gabby nods.

"The one for toddlers? Mrs. Wilson has been taking Matthias to those. She said he enjoys it."

Lacey nods. "That's the one. The woman who usually does it is having surgery."

"How long are you filling in?" Gabby asks.

Lacey ducks her head. "Two weeks."

"Do you think you could take Matti with you to the library since it's a short-term gig?" I ask, hoping that it works out. The more I get to know Lacey, the more perfect I think this arrangement might be.

Lacey nods. "I'm sure Samantha would be okay with that."

I grin. "Think about it," I say, trying not to beg. "Let me know. In the meantime, I'll ask around at work and see if anyone has any suggestions for someone to keep him on Monday if you are working."

Gabby bumps her hip into Lacey. "She'll let you know soon."

"Thanks. I need to go get Matti, but it was nice to meet you, Gabby. Lacey, I look forward to hearing from you soon. You have my card."

I give them both a small wave, and head into the diner to pick up my to-go order. Glancing at my watch, I have just enough time to get Matti from Mrs. Wilson and get back home in time to watch a baseball rerun before bed. Les was a huge baseball fan, and I want to make sure I expose Matti to that. So, while I don't know a thing about baseball yet, I'm determined to learn.

Chapter Six

Lacey

I WATCH AS KNOX walks quickly toward the parking area behind the diner. A low whistle grabs my attention.

"Well, you've been holding out," Gabby says, slipping her arm into mine and nudging me toward the square. "When did you meet that handsome man?"

I laugh. "He came into the coffee shop the other day."

"Mmhmm, and you didn't tell me about him because ..." She glances at me, one eyebrow raised.

"I don't tell you about every customer that comes into the shop, silly." I shake my head. "Besides, I didn't know he wasn't married until today."

She grins. "There it is!"

I can feel my cheeks turning pink. "Nah, you know I'm not looking for a relationship. I've got goals." I don't mention the curse.

Gabby knows my opinion on relationships, of course, but she thinks I'm way off base.

"Why can't you have both?" she asks, innocently.

"You know why," I say, stepping up to the light pole and pushing the button for the crosswalk.

"Don't tell me you still believe your family is cursed." She pins me with a hard stare. "You know that's bologna, right?"

I shrug. "No one in my family has managed to stay married. Especially once kids came into the picture." I come from a long line of single moms. I've seen and heard the stories. I never want to struggle like they did, and I never want my child to wonder why their father didn't want them.

"So, you've decided you'll never get married or have a family of your own based on everyone else's bad choices?"

The walk signal lights up. "Let's go," I say, pulling her across the street with me.

"This isn't over," she says, jogging to keep up with me.

"Sure it is," I say, grinning. "Unless you want to talk about Heath. Besides, I need to figure out if I can take this job or not."

"Of course you can." As soon as she hits the sidewalk, she leans over, placing her hands on her knees. "Please don't make me jog anymore. I'm not made for running."

I laugh. "Sorry, when my thoughts get going, my legs try to keep up."

She stands, and I slip my arm in hers. "Let's walk and talk. Slowly."

"So," Gabby says when she finally catches her breath. "What are you really afraid of?"

I glance around the square, marveling at how quickly the town council can remove all the Christmas decor once the holidays have passed.

Gabby catches her breath and sighs. "I miss the decorations already." She turns and faces me. "Really though, what are you afraid of?"

I suck in a deep breath. "I'm not afraid of anything. Well, maybe spiders and clowns."

Gabby stops and puts her hands on her hips. "Lacey, do I need to call Bryce and have him talk some sense into you?"

"You wouldn't," I say, pinning her with my best puppy dog eyes. "You know he hates that I work in a coffee shop. I'd never hear the end of this."

She shrugs. "You've got goals, Lacey. I want to see you reach them. If nannying for the oh-so-handsome Dr. Knox helps get you there, I'm not sure what the problem is."

My face flames red. Sweat breaks out on my forehead.

"Ohhh ..." Gabby grins. "You *are* attracted to him!"

I shake my head furiously. "No. I'm not."

"Then I don't see what the issue is. You could drop to two days a week, which you know Aurora won't mind because the busy season is over. Nanny for Knox and save up for the lease on the spot next to the Coffee Loft, you've had your eye on for months. I don't see how this could go wrong, honestly."

I can think of a million ways, actually, but I find myself agreeing with her. "Yeah. I'll talk to Aurora. Now, tell me, what's new with you?"

We spend the next hour walking around the square, window shopping and talking about Gabby's visits with Mrs. Atkins. She's visited once a week since the woman was diagnosed with cancer and her son, Heath, was deployed overseas.

"Promise you'll talk to Aurora and really think about this opportunity?" Gabby says as we reach my car.

"I will." I lean in and give her a hug. "Thanks for helping me sort through my thoughts."

Gabby squeezes me tight. "Anytime. Call me and let me know how the talk with her goes."

"I will." I get in my car and pull out of the parking spot. Glancing back, I see Gabby staring at something across the street. I look over, but whatever she saw must be gone, because the sidewalk is empty.

· · · · ·

My stomach churns as I glance at the clock on the wall. Two-thirty.

Aurora will be here any minute.

"Why do you look like you're going to throw up?" Ashlan asks, her hip leaning against the counter.

"Because, I might." I've been turning this over in my head since I left the town square Monday evening. "What if Aurora gets mad?"

"What if Aurora gets mad about what?" a voice says from behind me.

I spin and come face to face with my boss. "I ... uh ..."

Ashlan steps away from the counter. "How did you get in here and we didn't hear the bell chime?"

Aurora grins. "I came in through the back. So," she says, looking over to me again. "What is Aurora going to be mad about?" She raises her eyebrow.

"Well ..." I take a deep breath. "I was wondering if we could discuss my hours."

Aurora's face falls. "I'm sorry, Lacey. It's the slow season. I don't think I can give you any more hours right now."

I nod. "I know," I say. "I was actually wondering if I could reduce them a bit."

Aurora's eyes go wide. "Let's go in the office and talk," she says when the door chimes open behind her.

I follow her into the tiny office off the back of the coffee shop, and close the door.

"Have a seat," she says, motioning to the small chair beside the desk. She places her jacket on the hook, and then sits down in the chair behind the desk. "What kind of reduction are you asking for?"

I twist my hands in my lap. Deciding to share the whole story, I start at the beginning "You know I've been trying to save money to start my own children's education center."

She nods.

"Well, I was offered a position as a nanny, and the pay is ... well, it will help me get there a whole lot faster."

"Okay," she says. "So, are you turning in your notice?" Her face falls a bit. I've gotten to know Aurora really well since she bought the Coffee Loft.

"Oh, no. Nothing like that," I say in a rush. "I was just wondering if I could maybe drop Mondays. I can still be here for the Wednesday and Saturday shifts. At least until I've saved enough to snag the space next to this one for the center."

Aurora sits back in her chair and smiles. "We should be able to accommodate that. When are you looking to make the change? This week's schedule is already up."

Excitement bubbles in my stomach and I envision myself floating through the coffee shop like in the movies. "Not until next week," I say, trying to come back down to earth.

She takes out the paper calendar we use to track requests for time off and makes some notes. "I think that will be fine," she says.

"Thank you!" I stand to go back out to the front and finish my shift.

"Lacey, hold on," she says, causing me to pause. "You're looking to rent the space next to this one?"

I nod. "I think it would be perfect. Parents could pop in over here for a coffee before heading to the center. Moms come in here all the time with their little ones."

Aurora leans forward, placing her elbows on her desk. "And how much were you quoted for rent on that space?"

"To be honest, I haven't asked. The previous owner of this building was renting it out to the book shop for $15,000 a month. I just don't have that kind of capital saved to float me for six months while I establish a clientele."

She nods. "Do you have a business plan drawn up?"

"I do. I've got everything worked out." I sigh. "Now I just need the start-up funds."

"What about your brother?" she asks.

I shake my head. "No, he offered, but I declined. He was always giving things up for me when we were kids. I don't want to take his money now."

"I understand." Aurora smiles. "Bring in your business plan, and I'll take a look at it. Maybe we can get you that funding sooner rather than later. I've got some experience with this, you know."

I grin. "Thanks," I squeak.

"No problem," she grins. "For what it's worth, I think it's a great idea!"

Stepping outside the office, I quietly close the door. Once I'm sure it's shut, I do a silent scream and dance.

Things might finally be falling into place.

Chapter Seven

Knox

THE LIBRARY PARKING LOT is full of small children and their moms funneling inside. I glance in the rearview mirror and smile. Matti has both of his shoes in his hands, waving them around. I'm learning he doesn't like to leave his shoes on in the car.

"Ready for story time, Matti?" I ask, opening my door.

"Stories!" Matti squeals. "Colors."

I just smile as I open his door and slip his shoes back on before unbuckling his seat. "Do they color at story time?" I ask. Usually Mrs. Wilson is the one who brings Matthias to story time, but I'm off this morning, so I brought him. Besides, I'll get to see Lacey in action.

Not that she's the reason I'm here.

"Colors!" Matti yells as he tries to make a break for it as soon as his feet hit the ground.

"Matti, hold my hand, remember?" I ask, holding tight to his chubby fist. "No running in the parking lot."

Matti frowns. "I want to color!"

We walk inside the library hand in hand. Matti knows exactly where he's going, so I let him lead the way. He walks past the check-in desk to the colorful corner in the back with a cardboard cutout of a dragon reading a book.

As soon as we turn the corner into the children's area, I see a room off to the right with a colorful round rug in the center. Little tables and chairs take up the back section of the room. I let go of Matti's hand and he makes his way into the room, to the front of the rug, and sits.

Looking around, I notice the room is filled with women who are now staring at me. I give a little wave and find an open seat against the wall near the door—just in case Matti tries to make a break for it.

A few moments later, Lacey enters, a stack of books in her hands.

"Hey," I say, getting her attention. She jumps a bit at the sound of my voice, and her stack of books falls to the ground.

"Oh no!" She kneels on the floor and starts picking up the fallen items.

"I'm sorry," I say, joining her on the floor. "I didn't mean to startle you."

"It's okay." She blows a lock of blue hair away from her eyes. "I just wasn't expecting to see you here."

"I brought—" Several children squealing at once interrupts my sentence.

"I better get going." Lacey stands and quickly makes her way to the front of the room. "I'm sorry I'm late," she says to the waiting group of kids. "The book dragon and I couldn't find the right story for today."

Gasps and giggles fill the space.

"Are we ready to hear a story?" she asks the kids.

"Yeah!" the kids shout, turning to face the front of the room where a chair is set up for Lacey.

She walks past the chair, and sits on the floor with the kids.

I sit and watch as Lacey begins reading the first story. She makes all the voices, pauses in the right places, and has each of the children engaged. By the end, I realize I've been just as enthralled with her storytelling.

"Color time!" Matti yells when Lacey directs them to the small table in the back.

"Actually," she says over the commotion of small bodies pulling out chairs and getting settled. "I thought we would do a science experiment."

"Color!" Matti yells again.

Lacey calmly squats down on his level. "Today we are going to try something new, okay?"

"No!" Before I squeeze between the moms who are now staring openly at Matti, he stands, flipping his chair backwards, and bolts for the door.

"Matti!" I call, wriggling my way out from the wall of moms. "Matti, wait!"

Matti is out the door and into the children's section in a flash. I'm chasing a not-quite-three-year-old.

Through a library.

Whisper-yelling for him to stop.

This cannot be my life.

Finally, just as Matti rounds the check-out desk, an older gentleman steps out and swoops him up. "Where ya going, little fella?"

"I want to color!" Matti sobs, tears falling down his reddened cheeks.

"Okay," says the older man. "I bet your dad can help you with that." He turns so Matti can see me. I'd love for the ground to open up and swallow me whole. I'm not sure I've ever felt so out of my element in my life.

"Not my daddy," Matti cries. He kicks his legs and wriggles with all his might to get free.

"It's a long story," I say to the older man who is now eyeing me suspiciously. "I'm his uncle. My sister and her husband recently passed away."

He nods. "I see." Gently he passes the still-upset Matti to me. "Give it time, son." He pats my arm and gives me a sad smile.

"I want to color," Matti whimpers as he lays his head on my shoulder.

"I know," I say. I rub his back and head back to the story time room to get the cup and keys I left under the chair I was sitting in. "Let me get our things, and we can go home and color."

I step inside the room and I'm immediately surrounded by the moms.

"Oh my gosh, he's a handful," one of the women says, batting her eyelashes. "If you ever need an extra set of hands to help out, I'd be happy to join you."

I glance at her hand. No ring. "Thanks, but I think I'm all set." I have no intention of getting involved with someone right now. My eyes slide to Lacey who's busy helping with the activity she had planned, and I hesitate. I shake my head, clearing it of any thoughts of Lacey and me holding hands and walking behind Matti through a park. My focus is, and needs to be, on Matthias.

"Well, here's my number in case you change your mind," she says, slipping a piece of paper into my hand. A couple of other women give words of encouragement, along with their numbers and instructions to call anytime. Seriously? I didn't think story time was where single parents went to pick up dates. Guess I have a lot to learn.

I grab the cup and car keys and make my way over to where Lacey is standing, watching the kids. "I'm so sorry," I say when I finally catch her attention.

"It's okay," she says, grinning. "It happens ..."

I groan. "Don't say it."

She laughs and turns her attention to Matthias. "Hey there, Matti. How about next week I'll make sure there's paper and crayons for coloring? Just in case."

Matti nods and presses his head into my shoulder.

"I know you're busy right now," I say, motioning to the table full of busy children. "But I'd love to talk to you about the nanny position when you have some time."

She nods. "I was going to call you this afternoon."

I grin. "Great, can I make you lunch? I'd offer to buy you lunch, but I have a feeling Matti's going to take a longer nap today."

"Sure," she says, brushing Matti's hair out of his face. "I'll call you when I'm done here."

I turn to leave the room and catch the eyes of the women who were so quick to offer their help. They are scowling and talking to each other in hushed tones. I fight not to roll my eyes. "Let's go, Matti," I say, cuddling him closer to my chest.

Chapter Eight

Lacey

I SHOULD HAVE EXPECTED things to go wrong today when I woke up twenty minutes late. Apparently, I set my alarm for eight o'clock at night instead of eight in the morning. I'd planned to be at the library early, to have all the books and supplies in place, and be ready to go before the first family arrived.

Oh, to dream. Instead, I was rushing in at the last minute when the sound of Knox's voice startled me and I dropped everything. Thankfully, I salvaged the rest of story time, save Matti being upset about the change of plans. I hadn't anticipated that the kids would already have a routine established. I should have asked. I chalk it up to being my first time filling in for story time.

Matti had expected time to color, and I hadn't planned for that. I tuck that away to think about. I'll have to make sure that anyone who volunteers or works at my center is prepared if a child needs an alternate plan for the activity. Maybe I can have an art station set up in the back of the room.

I'm cleaning up the last of the tables from our salt and watercolor experiment, when I overhear two moms talking as they buckle their little ones into strollers. I'm trying not to eavesdrop, when I hear "blue hair" and "deserves better" in the same sentence. I pause and hold my breath, watching my dreams go up in flames. If these moms don't enjoy the things I have lined up for next week, they could make it difficult for me to launch my children's center.

The drawbacks of living in a small-town.

"Can you believe he'd invite her to lunch? He's a doctor for goodness' sake."

I frown. On the one hand, at least they aren't talking about the class.

"Besides, how would someone with her style fit in with him?"

I glance down at my oversized t-shirt and yoga pants. I'd thrown on something comfortable to get on the ground with the kids and read.

Tears prick the back of my eyes. Maybe I was wrong to come back home to this small-town. Bryce had asked me to go with him to Colorado, but in hockey, there's no guarantee where you'll be living long term. Besides, I've always loved Piney Brook. I couldn't imagine living so far away from Mom.

I throw the remaining trash in the bin and gather the books to put back on the shelves before I leave.

The two women leave the small room first, casting a glance back in my direction. Such a middle school thing to do, really. I shouldn't let it bother me, but it does.

When I went off to college, I decided to experiment with my hair. Different colors, cuts, styles. It makes me happy to try something new.

My free hand finds a lock of blue hair and twirls it. When Anna, my hair stylist, wanted to try a new color, I was excited. Now I'm wondering if it's too much.

"How did it go?" Samantha asks, stepping out from behind the circulation desk and taking half the stack of books. "The kids seemed happy as they were leaving."

I shrug. "It seemed to go okay," I say, averting my gaze.

"Okay, spill it. What happened?" Samantha motions for me to join her in the children's section to reshelve the books.

"Apart from Matti running out screaming, you mean?" I ask, giving her a half smile.

She nods. "That happens. They're little kids."

"Knox asked me over to lunch to discuss a job opportunity, and some of the moms overheard." I slide the first book into its spot on the shelf.

"Okay ..."

"Apparently, someone with blue hair isn't good enough to be with someone like him." The words taste like acid in my mouth.

"Uh huh." Samantha slides her last book onto the shelf. "And what do you think?"

I turn and lean my hip against the bookcase. "I think hair isn't what makes someone ugly."

She laughs so hard she snorts. "You're absolutely right."

"Thanks, Samantha."

She pats my arm. "No problem. See you next week?"

I nod. "I'll be here."

I gather my things from behind her desk and walk out into the sunshine. I pull my phone out from my bag, and locate the card Knox gave me from the bottom of my bag. Punching in the numbers, I take a breath and hit dial.

"Hello," Knox answers after the second ring.

"Hey, it's Lacey." My voice quivers, but I hope he doesn't hear it.

"Hey, I've been waiting for your call. Matti is just finishing up his last coloring page and then we'll be ready for lunch. Are you still okay to join us? I make a mean macaroni and cheese."

I hesitate. The conversation from before ringing in my ears.

"If you don't like mac and cheese, I can throw in some dinosaur chicken nuggets. I'll even give you all the T-Rex ones." He laughs. "I'm living on toddler food right now. I never know what he will like from one meal to the next."

I chuckle. "Mac and cheese is fine. Text me your address?" I'm not going to let some gossipy moms ruin my chances at opening my own center. If this job is what it takes to get me there, nothing and no one will stand in my way.

*   *   *   *   *

I'm halfway to Knox's house when I find myself stopped in the middle of the road. Someone's dog is roaming free. I push the button for my hazards, and open the car door.

Slowly, I approach the dog. My hands out in front of me, I step a little closer, talking softly. "Come on. It's okay. You must be cold." The dog cowers in the middle of the road. "Come on, let's get you warm."

Slowly, the dog makes its way to my outstretched hands. She's so dirty, it's hard to tell what breed she is. Gently I coax her to my car and open the back door. Finally, she hops inside. I get back into the driver's seat and turn up the heat. Poor girl is shivering. And thin.

I pull the car off the side of the road where we will be a little safer, and call Knox.

"Hello?"

"Hey, I'm sorry. I'm going to have to ask for a rain check." A small yip sounds from the back seat of my car.

"Do you have a dog with you?" Knox asks.

"Well, I was on my way to your house when I came across a stray dog in the road. I couldn't just leave her there in the cold." I reach back to give her a reassuring pat.

"You have a strange dog in your car?" Knox sounds concerned.

"She's not strange, Knox. She's lost. Or she's been dumped. Either way, she needs my help."

"I get it," he says softly. "Where are you taking her?"

"Piney Brook Animal Hospital. I'm not sure if they are still working half days or if they're back to their regular hours." I feel my forehead crease as I consider my options.

"And if they're closed?"

"I'll have to cross that bridge when I get to it."

"Do you need help?" Knox asks. "I can put Matti in the car and come to you."

I pull the phone away from my face for a second. *Did he really just offer to come help me?* Mom and Bryce would have told me to call animal control and leave it be.

"No, thanks. I've got it. Thanks for offering, though. I'm sure Matti would rather nap in his own bed, and he's already had an eventful morning."

"Okay, keep me posted," Knox says. "And, Lacey, be careful."

"Will do," I say before hanging up the phone.

I pull the car back out onto the road and hang a left. Ten minutes later, I'm sitting in the car staring at the closed sign on the front door of the vet's office.

"Well, that answers that," I say to Flower lying comfortably in the back seat. She doesn't seem to mind that I've decided to call her Flower, or that I have no idea what to do next.

"Now what?"

Chapter Nine

Knox

MATTI AND I SHARED a lunch of boxed macaroni and cheese and his favorite—for now—dinosaur-shaped chicken nuggets, with apple slices, and I put him down for a nap. I glance out the window at the brown lawn, courtesy of winter, and sigh.

I wonder if the vet's office was able to help Lacey with the stray she picked up. Deciding to call her and ask, I snag my phone off the coffee table and sink into the couch.

After dialing her number, I press send and wait.

"Hello?" She sounds slightly out of breath and frazzled.

"Hey, Lacey? It's Knox. Are you okay?"

"Wait! Hold on! Be still for a minute would ya?" Her words are muffled a bit, and a clatter makes me think she dropped the phone.

"Lacey? Lacey, are you okay?" Suddenly, I'm worried.

"Hang on! I dropped the phone." Her voice sounds distant and she is definitely distracted. "Flower! No, don't jump ..." There's a rustling noise, and then her voice is suddenly clear. "Sorry about that. I was trying to give Flower a bath."

"Flower?" I ask, unsure what she's talking about. "Who is Flower?"

She giggles. "The dog, silly."

"The dog from the road?"

"Yes, she stank. I can't have a stinky dog in the house. My mom would kick us both out."

Suddenly, I realize I have no idea how old Lacey is. "Um, Lacey?"

"Yeah?"

"How old are you?"

She huffs. "I'm twenty-four, plenty old enough to be a nanny. I finished college two years ago with high marks. Do you want a copy of my transcripts?"

"No, I was just curious." I stumble over my words. *Should I ask her for her transcripts?* I hadn't even considered that. I'd been so happy to find someone who seemed qualified to watch Matti, I didn't even think about verifying her qualifications.

"Okay, well." She pauses. "I'd understand if you did. It's a big thing to hire someone to care for your child. Even if you aren't the biological father, you're all he has now. It would make sense."

I let out a sigh of relief. "Honestly, I'm new at this. I have no idea what I'm doing, but I'm pretty sure I'm doing it all wrong."

She laughs. "Trust me, you can't be doing everything wrong. You care—that much is evident."

"So," I start. "If I were to officially be interviewing you, what kinds of questions would I ask?"

She spends the next few minutes talking about the qualifications I should look for in a nanny or caregiver. "Just in case I don't work out," she finishes.

"Oh, okay. That makes sense." My ears are ringing from all of the things she mentioned. *How do parents do this*? "I'd like to reschedule lunch if we could. I'd like Matthias to see you in our home, and for you to get comfortable here as well."

"That sounds good to me," she says. A crash sounds in the background. "Flower! Goodness, you're making a huge mess. Hang on, Knox."

Before I can agree, the sound from the other end muffles. She must have put the phone down on something soft.

"Sorry, Flower knocked over the potted plant, and I had to clean it up." She sighs. "I don't know what I'm going to do with you."

"With me?" I ask, confused.

"No." She laughs. "With Flower."

"Oh, I thought you were taking him to the animal hospital?"

"I was," she sighs. "But they were closed and *she* needs a warm place to sleep tonight."

"I see. And why is her name Flower?"

She giggles, the sound lighting me up from the inside like a Christmas tree topper. "Because she was stinky. It reminded me of the skunk in the movie Bambi."

I grin. "Ah, that makes sense."

"I should be able to drop her off tomorrow, but it breaks my heart thinking that she may go into a shelter. She's such a sweet dog."

There's a hint of longing in her voice, and it gets me right in the gut. "There's no way you can keep her?"

"No, not with the hours I'll be working. Who would walk her? Who would she sleep with at night?"

"Oh," I say, mulling that over. "Would it help if you brought her with you to watch Matti?" *What? What in the world did I just offer?*

She squeals. "Really?"

"Well, as long as he's ... I'm sorry, *she's* good with Matti, I don't see why not." In for a penny, in for a pound, as they say.

"I could just kiss you right now!" She squeals again. "I mean, not really. You're my boss. Kind of. Not that I wouldn't kiss you. I mean ..."

I laugh. "It's okay, Lacey. I know what you meant."

"Great! So, I'll take Flower to the vet tomorrow and make sure she's healthy and then we can schedule a meet and greet so that Matti and Flower can get to know each other." She takes a deep breath.

I'd be out of breath too if I was talking a mile a minute.

"How does that sound?" she asks.

"Sure," I say, smiling. "Sounds like a plan."

The sound of breaking glass makes me cringe.

"You don't have anything breakable down low do you?"

I glance around my sister's house. It's pretty toddler proof, but would that matter with a dog? I make a note to look up dog-proofing a house when we hang up.

"I'll make sure it's all clear," I say.

"Uncle Knox," Matti shouts from his room. "I wake up now."

"I've got to run. Matthias is awake. I work tomorrow, but just send me a text for a day and time that work for you after Flower is cleared by the vet."

A thunk followed by a loud cry sounds from down the hallway. I hit end on the phone, and toss it onto the couch before dashing down the hallway towards Matti's room.

I swing open the door, and find Matti sprawled across the floor, crying. "Matti, buddy. How'd you get out of your crib?" I glare at the furniture that was supposed to keep him safely contained.

"I cyimb," he cries.

I pick him up and hold him close to me. "Are you okay?"

He continues crying and shaking his head no. Adrenaline shoots through my body, and I stand with him in my arms. "Let's go get you checked out," I say, rubbing his back as I slide my feet into a pair of flip flops I'd left by the front door.

An hour and some teasing from the ER staff later, we are back home. Matti is fine, but the pediatrician did suggest moving him to a toddler bed. Matti and I are cuddled on the couch, watching his favorite movie about talking race cars, and I am flipping through my phone looking at options for toddler beds.

I'd thought being an ER doctor was an adventure. Nothing prepared me for moving to Piney Brook and becoming Matthias's guardian.

Chapter Ten

Lacey

GETTING FLOWER BACK INTO my car this morning was a challenge. Apparently, she knows a good house when she destroys one. My mom took one look at the broken flower pot and busted fruit bowl and went right to her room for the rest of the night, but not before requesting I find Flower a new home.

Immediately.

"Ms. Chambers?" A young woman with sandy blonde hair and bright red lipstick enters the exam room. "I'm Dr. Brewer. Who do we have here?"

Flower raises her head and looks at Dr. Brewer before licking my hand and trying to squeeze between my legs.

"This is Flower. I found her in the middle of the road yesterday afternoon. She was covered in leaves and dirt. Smelled to high heaven."

Dr. Brewer washes her hands and sits down on the ground in front of Flower. "I see. We'll scan her for a microchip, and see if anything comes up." She reaches her hand out slowly, and Flower leans her nose forward to sniff it. "We'll also run some labs and make sure she's healthy."

"Thanks," I say. I hadn't considered someone might be looking for her. I'd assumed she was out in the wild on her own. What if there's a family waiting for her? I run my hand down Flower's silky coat. "I'd appreciate that."

After several pokes, prods, and scans, it's determined that Flower doesn't have a microchip after all. Of course, that doesn't mean she's not someone's pet.

"Would you be interested in fostering her while we look for her family?" Dr. Brewer asks. "She's pretty healthy, all things considered. Though she is a bit underweight."

"What would that mean?" I ask, hesitantly. I could see myself getting attached to Flower, and then having to let her go. It might break my heart.

"Well, you'd take her home and care for her. We'd put ads out, and post on area social media sites, to see if we can locate her owners."

"And if you can't?"

Dr. Brewer smiles. "If we can't, you'd have first right of adoption."

I grin. "She wouldn't need to stay at the shelter?"

The doctor shakes her head. "She's healthy and friendly, so no."

I nod my head. "I'll do it." Hopefully, Mom will come around. Besides, Knox said I could bring her with me when I'm watching Matti. Piece of cake. Right?

"Great! That is so much better for her than sending her to the shelter to wait." Dr. Brewer makes a note in her chart. "We'll contact you if we find her owners." She hands me a stack of papers outlining the care that Flower needs. "Call us if you have any questions."

I nod, and she smiles before walking out of the room.

"Well, Flower. I guess we hurry up and wait."

We leave the animal hospital, and I head to the Coffee Loft. I'm usually off on Fridays, so this was the perfect time to find a lost dog in the middle of the road, right?

I pull into the parking space in front of the older brick building and sigh. I love this town. The historic downtown area still looks the same as it did hundreds of years ago. I'm sure some things have changed, but the bones are the same, anyway. It's part of what brought me back home after college. I couldn't imagine living in a big city without the charm and character of Piney Brook.

"Hey!" Ashlan exclaims when I poke my head through the door.

"Hey! Do you want to meet Flower?" I ask, careful to keep the pup outside.

"You know I do!" Ashlan comes around the counter. "Let me get Aurora. You know she loves dogs."

The two women step out the front door a few minutes later, oohing and ahhing over Flower.

"I've always wanted a dog of my own," Aurora says. "I just work too much."

I nod my head. "I know. I wanted one growing up, but my mom didn't feel like I'd be responsible enough. Then I was leaving for college and she didn't want to have an animal to take care of."

Ashlan frowns. "Really? I had all kinds of pets growing up. We had dogs, cats, hamsters ... heck, one time I even had a tarantula."

I shiver. "No way!"

"Yep," she nods her head. "It was cute, too. All furry. Until it got out of its cage and my momma sucked it up with the vacuum cleaner."

I hold in my laugh, knowing I'd have done the same thing. Ashlan looks positively sad about the ordeal though.

"Are you keeping her?" Aurora asks, changing the subject from spiders.

"Dr. Brewer is going to look for her owners. She's going to make sure some family isn't missing her right now. If not, I'm gonna try and talk my mom into letting me keep her."

"How will you have the time for her?" Ashlan asks, rubbing her silky brown fur.

"Knox said I can bring her along when I watch Matti, so that just leaves my Coffee Loft shifts that she'll be at home. I think that should be okay. I borrowed a crate from the vet, so that should help, too."

Ashlan and Aurora exchange a look. "Knox seems nice," Aurora says carefully.

I raise a brow. "Uh huh. And?"

"He's handsome, and he's obviously a family man if he moved here to take care of his nephew."

I nod. "That's true. I'm sure he'll make a decent boss."

Ashlan laughs. "Don't you ever read romance novels?"

I shrug my shoulders. "Cursed, remember? Happily-ever-afters like that only happen in novels. That kind of stuff doesn't exist in real life. At least, not for me."

She giggles. "We'll see. I've been telling you for years, that curse is a bunch of nonsense."

"How else would you explain three generations of divorced single moms?" I ask, putting my hands on my hips.

"Bad choices in men? Different times?" Aurora offers. "Just because something didn't work for others doesn't mean it can't work for you. You learn from their mistakes and make better choices."

I frown. "I don't follow."

"Seeing their struggle has helped you learn what you don't want, right?"

"Well, sure, but I can't imagine they set out to have the life they did either," I argue.

"No, I'm sure not. But things were different for them. It only takes one person to break a generational pattern." Aurora looks at me, her big brown eyes staring deep into mine. Almost like she is willing this idea to take root in my brain.

"Yeah, well. I'd rather not test that theory. But you're right about me breaking the pattern—that's what I'm doing by staying out of relationships, and not having a kid."

An older couple approaches the doorway from the sidewalk and smiles at Flower. "How sweet," the woman says. "Do you mind if we bother you? We'd love a cappuccino."

Ashlan moves to open the door for the couple. "Of course, right this way. Just let me wash my hands."

Aurora puts her hand on my shoulder. "I hope you see things can be different. Otherwise, you might miss out on something great." She turns and walks into the Coffee Loft, leaving me standing on the sidewalk with a drooling Flower.

Chapter Eleven

Knox

THE EMERGENCY ROOM IS busy today. Who knew January was the best time to clean out gutters or trim tree limbs? I certainly wouldn't have advised Old Mr. Thomas to do it himself. That's for sure.

The septuagenarian is certainly fit for his age. Or he was until the fall from the ladder broke his hip. His wife, Martha, rode in the ambulance with him holding his hand. It's sweet to see an older couple still in love.

"Mr. Thomas, I have some bad news." I say, stepping into his room.

"Don't tell me," he says, shaking his head. "Just tell me when I can get back home." He waves off Mrs. Thomas who is wiping a cloth across his forehead. "My Martha can't take care of the house alone, ya see."

I nod. "I'm sorry. You've broken your hip. That's going to require surgery."

He sighs. "How long?"

Martha squeezes his hand. "It'll be all right, dear."

"You'll be in the hospital for a few days, but you'll need help around the house for several weeks. I suggest going to a rehab facility after you're released from here."

"Can't," he says. "I've never been away from Martha that long." He wipes his eyes.

"Unless you can find or hire someone to help you at home, I really do recommend a rehab facility. Either way, you'll need physical therapy."

"Fine." He looks at his wife.

"We'll figure something out, dear," she says, patting his hand.

"I'm sorry," I say again. "The surgeon will be around soon to talk to you both. Do you need anything?"

Mr. Thomas shakes his head.

I step out of the room to give them some privacy to digest what they've just heard. This part of the job is hard. I want to offer to step in and help them, but it's not feasible or ethical. Besides, I'm still treading water with Matti.

A few hours later, the floor is finally quiet. I'm finishing my notes on the computer when Briella steps up beside me.

"I've heard a rumor, doc," she says, grinning from ear to ear.

"If it's that I brought my nephew in when he fell out of his crib, that's old news," I say, trying to head off any more embarrassing teasing. Of course, I could have done a concussion protocol at home, but I was too emotional. I couldn't think when he was hurt.

"Not that," she says. "That's perfectly normal. Everyone's just giving you a hard time because they can." She grins. "Sheila, from the peds department upstairs, brought her son in last summer when he fell and skinned his knees. It's hard to be objective when it's your baby who's hurt."

I sit back in the chair, thinking about what she's just shared. "Thanks, Briella. That does make me feel a little better."

"So ..." She waggles her eyebrows. "Talk in the mom's group online is that you have a thing for a certain blue-haired beauty."

I laugh and shake my head. "A thing? What is this, middle school?"

"Well, do you?" she asks, rubbing her hands together like she can't wait to confirm or deny the gossip.

"I've asked her to nanny for me. That's all," I say, holding my hands up in front of me.

She pouts. "Darn, I was hoping to knock those nosy moms down a peg."

I frown. "What do you mean?"

"There were some moms who were saying how a smart, attractive doctor like yourself couldn't possibly find a blue-haired coffee girl attractive." She scowls. "As if they know anything about Lacey."

"What?" I ask, dumbfounded. "How in the world would anyone know anything about what I like in a woman? I've been at work or with Matti since I moved here."

She shakes her head. "The rumor mill in a small-town works overtime when a newcomer is deemed up for grabs."

"Up for—" I sigh, and rub my hands over my face. "Good grief. It really is like middle school."

Briella chuckles. "Mostly, it's just fun and gossip, but the things they were saying about Lacey got me riled up."

"How well do you know Lacey?" I ask.

"We went to school together all our lives. She's good people." Briella's tone leaves no room for argument. "If you want the best of the best to be Matti's nanny, you couldn't have picked a better person."

I nod. "Thanks."

Briella tilts her head to the side and eyes me. "You sure you don't think she's attractive?"

My mouth falls open in shock. "I never said that." I sputter. "She's a beautiful young woman, and caring ..."

Briella grins and throws her hands in the air. "Yes! I was right."

"Huh?" I ask, more confused than ever.

She just grins and turns to walk away. "Have a great night, Dr. Sullivan."

I sit for a moment, replaying the conversation over in my head. I have a feeling Briella is up to something. Glancing at the clock on the wall I get back to work. I'm due to pick up Matti from Mrs. Wilson's, and she won't be pleased if I'm late.

꧁ ꧁ ꧁ ꧁ ꧁

The bright sunshine peeks through the gap in the curtains I clearly didn't pull closed last night. I roll to my side and open my eyes, only to let out a scream. Matti startles and starts to cry. Get a toddler bed they said. It will be safer, they said. *Until I have a heart attack.*

I lean off the edge of the bed, and pick Matti up. Pulling him into the bed with me, I try to soothe him. "I'm sorry, Matti. You scared me. How long were you standing there?"

Matti sniffles and shrugs. "I hungy."

I look at the alarm clock on the nightstand—seven a.m. Great. "Me too," I say, stretching my arms above my head and yawning. "How about we make pancakes?"

Matti shakes his head.

"No pancakes today? Okay then, eggs?"

Matti shakes his heads again. "Chocat milk and biscuit."

I stare at him a minute, hoping that he changes his mind to something easier. "I don't think we have biscuits."

He shakes his head again and walks to the door. "Bye-bye."

"You want to go bye-bye and get chocolate milk and a biscuit?"

Matti nods and claps his hands together.

"Okay," I say, wondering where I can get him a biscuit and chocolate milk at seven o'clock on a Saturday morning.

"Chocat milk!" He's still clapping his hands with glee.

I grin. "I understand what you want!" I squeeze him to me and hold him tight. "Let's get dressed."

I release him and Matti hops off the bed and runs into his room. I step inside his bedroom and see him struggling to get his head through a shirt he picked. "Need some help?" I ask, sitting on the floor and waiting for his response.

"No, I do it!"

He struggles for another minute before giving up. "Help pease."

"I'll always be here to help, Matthias. Anytime you ask." I help him get his head through the correct hole, and slip his other arm through as well. Pulling the striped shirt over his belly, I grin. "Great job! You almost had it. You'll be dressing yourself in no time."

"I a big boy!" He grabs his pants and slips them on with minimal struggle.

"Yes, you are," I say. It's moments like these I miss my sister the most. I know she would have wanted to see her baby boy be able to dress himself. I shake off the sadness and smile. "I'm going to get dressed and we'll be ready to go."

Matti nods and picks up his socks. His little tongue sticking out as he works to get one on his foot.

I laugh to myself, as I walk away to get ready to go.

Twenty minutes later, the smell of fresh coffee tingles my nose as we walk into the Coffee Loft. I inhale deeply. Maybe the caffeine will kick in quicker that way.

"Chocat milk!" Matti says excitedly as we move toward the front of the line.

"Hi there," a woman with curly auburn hair says. "What can I get you?"

I look around, but I don't see Lacey. I give the woman—Aurora, according to her name tag—our order and take Matti over to the corner booth.

We settle in, and I pull some paper and a pack of crayons out of the diaper bag. Matti's just started to color—I'm guessing a tree from the green glob on the top of the paper—when I notice someone coming to the table from the corner of my eye.

"Here's your order," a familiar voice says as a tray slides across our table.

"Bue!" Matti giggles.

"Hey," I say, a smile breaking out across my face. "I didn't think you were in today."

She laughs. "I was in the back grabbing some to-go lids. I meant to text you yesterday, but the day got away from me." She blushes. "When do you want to redo our meeting?"

I open Matti's chocolate milk and put his blueberry scone in front of him. "Well, we're free this evening. Would you like to join us for dinner?"

Someone at a nearby table begins to make choking sounds. I turn and spot the overly helpful mom from the library. Her face is red and flushed, but she's caught her breath again. *Was she eavesdropping?* I recall what Briella said yesterday and frown.

Lacey turns away from the scowling woman and smiles. "I'd love to."

I'm not sure if it's what Briella said, or if I'm just seeing Lacey clearly for the first time, but she really is stunning. Her blue-green eyes look like I could fall into them and spend a day leisurely swimming about. "I can't wait," I say a bit breathlessly.

Get it together, man. She's going to be your nanny, for goodness' sake.

Chapter Twelve

Lacey

I RUSH STRAIGHT HOME after work to change and check on Flower. The borrowed crate from the vet's office is the only reason my mom agreed to let her stay a few days. As soon as I hit the front door, my heart drops.

"Oh no," I groan. The door has a gaping hole where the mail slot used to be. Tears prick the back of my eyes. "Flower," I call as I open the door that my parents will definitely make me replace. "Flower, come here girl," I cringe as I look around the house. It appears Flower has figured out how to get into the pantry. Crushed chips, a ripped-open bag of marshmallows, and a chewed up … "Is that my shoe?" I shriek, and Flower dips back behind the arm of the couch where she's clearly been hiding.

I take a deep breath and remind myself that Flower is a girl used to living on the streets. She can't help that she ate my shoe and destroyed the house. The real question is, how did she escape the crate?

I do my best to clean up the mess while Flower spends some time in the backyard. Thankfully, it's winter, so my mom's prized flowers aren't in bloom to be destroyed. Once the mess is mostly cleaned up, I move to the front door. Sighing, I grab the vacuum to suck up all the little wooden shards that Flower managed to tear off the door, then I get some cardboard from the recycle bin and tape it over the gaping hole.

I grab my phone out of my pocket and hit dial.

"Hello?" My brother's deep voice is like a balm to my racing heart.

"Hey, bro," I say in what I'm hoping is a nonchalant tone.

"What did you do?" he asks. Bryce is older than me by two years, but you'd think it was a decade the way he babies me.

"Nothing," I stammer. "Okay, fine. So I may have rescued a dog. Who may have eaten some things from the pantry."

"May have?" Bryce asks. "Seriously, Lacey. What were you thinking? You know Mom's not a pet person."

I sigh and rub my forehead where pressure is starting to build. "You don't want a dog do you?"

He laughs. "Lace, you know I've always wanted a dog, but I can't take that on right now. When we aren't traveling, I'm at the practice facility training and skating."

Bryce is a hockey player for the Denver Edge. As soon as he could skate and hold a stick, he knew what he wanted to do with the rest of his life. It took me a little longer to figure it out. While he's traveling and living his dream, I'm here living with Mom.

"Lacey Marie Chambers!"

My shoulders reach for my ears in defense of my poor eardrums at the decibel of my mother's voice. "I'm going to replace it," I call out.

"Whoa, replace what?" Bryce asks, clearly catching on that there's a bigger problem than some stolen pantry items. "Do you need money, Lacey? I can transfer some to you right now."

"That mutt ate my door!"

I turn and face my mom. Her face is a shade of red I've only ever seen on a tomato. "Gotta go," I whisper to Bryce and hang up the phone, tossing it onto the couch.

Oh boy. "I promise. I'll replace it. I have no idea how she got out of the crate." My phone dings with an incoming text. I go to reach for it, but stop myself.

Mom turns and pins me with a look I've only seen once before, when Bryce and his friends thought it would be funny to try and stick their tongues to a frozen light pole outside. They'd seen it in a Christmas movie and had double-dog-dared each other to give it a go. Apparently, tongues really do stick. Who knew?

"I ..."

Mom holds up her hand and shakes her head, her auburn curls bouncing from side to side. "No. I don't want to hear it. You'll call someone to replace this door ASAP, and the dog will find a new home. Tonight."

I nod. "I'll call someone to fix the door, but, please, can't we have just a bit more time? I'm off tomorrow; I won't let her out of my sight." I know I'm begging, but my heart hurts thinking about dropping her off at a shelter. With a little love and some training, she'd be the perfect pet.

"No way," Mom says, already heading to her room.

I sigh and grab my phone from where I tossed it onto the couch. Knox is probably going to fire me from a job I don't even have yet. I wouldn't blame him.

Knox answers on the second ring. "Hello?"

"Hey," I say, forcing some pep into my voice. "Are you still okay with me bringing Flower tonight?"

"Of course," Knox says, clearing his throat. "I'm hoping that you and Matti will have some time to get to know each other and that he can meet Flower since you'll be bringing her along when you watch him."

"About that. I'm going to have to find her a new home."

"Oh, why?" he asks.

"Well," I say, taking a deep breath. "Flower had a bit of an accident today, and ..."

"An accident?" Knox asks, his voice soft with concern.

"Well, a misunderstanding, maybe? I don't know how to explain it."

"How about you tell me what happened and we go from there." Knox sounds so confident and sincere it breaks down the last of my defenses.

"She escaped the crate, raided the pantry, and tried to chew her way through the front door. She ate one of my shoes, and I can't keep her anymore. My mom is not a pet person, and Flower's obviously overstayed her welcome." Tears flow down my cheeks now.

"Oh," he says softly.

"I've always wanted a dog. When I was little, my mom said no every time I asked, and listed reasons just like this as to why." I sniffle and wipe my nose on my sleeve. "I'll have to drop her off at the shelter, but they're already full. I hate to think of what will happen to her. She just needs some training and some love. She deserves it."

Knox is quiet while I catch my breath. "Okay, I'll see you both soon, then?" he asks.

"Wait, what?"

"Well, you can't leave Flower at home alone, that much is clear. And you're not going to solve the problem in the next hour. I don't mind if you bring her over here. Two sets of eyes are better than one, and who knows, Matti might even enjoy petting her. Maybe we can come up with a plan for Flower together."

"Thank you," I say softly.

"You're welcome, Lacey. Don't forget her dishes and leash," Knox says before saying bye and hanging up.

I go collect Flower from the backyard where thankfully she's just chilling in a patch of grass sunning herself. "C'mon girl, let's get ready to go."

Flower slowly stretches as she gets to her feet, and then trots up to me, rubbing her head on my legs. My heart squeezes. I hope she gets adopted fast, and doesn't spend too much time at the shelter.

After a quick shower and change, I grab her things and clip on her leash. "I'm leaving with Flower," I call down the hallway.

"Good, I hope she finds a good home, but it can't be here," Mom says, sticking her head out of her doorway. "I'm sorry, I'm just not a pet person. You can have a dog when you move out."

I nod. "I know. I'm sorry for the trouble."

She smiles. "You've got a big heart. Sometimes it gets you in trouble, but you wouldn't be you without it."

"Thanks, Mom."

After bribing Flower with a treat to get back into the car, I punch Knox's address into the GPS and back out of the driveway. It's not a long drive. Knox lives just on the other side of town, near the hospital actually. Interesting.

I pull into the driveway of a ranch-style home. The soft gray paint and red brick make it a standout on the street. "Wow," I say to Flower. "This is nice."

Carefully, I get her out of the car and grab her dishes. I shut the car door, and let her sniff around in the yard. Surprisingly, she's good on a leash. It makes me wonder if she is someone's dog, after all. Maybe she Houdinied her way out of her home and went on an adventure.

I stop in my tracks. Maybe there's a little girl who's missing her dog. I look down at Flower and smile. "Do you have a family, girl?" I'll have to call Dr. Brewer and see if they've found an owner yet.

The front door swings open, and Knox stands in the doorway. My breath catches as the light from behind him illuminates his features. His kind eyes catch mine and he smiles. Tap-dancing gnomes start their jig in my stomach. *Oh no. No, no, no! You can't like your boss!*

Flower must have decided we'd waited long enough, because she shoots forward, yanking me off my feet, and sends me flying. I lose her leash and land sprawled face down on the lawn.

"Whoa!" Knox says, jumping down the few steps and grabbing her leash. "It's not nice to jerk your friend down," he admonishes.

Flower just bounces on her feet, slobbering and grinning. Well, as much as dogs grin, anyway.

"Sorry," I say, standing and brushing the dirt and grass off my clothes. "I wasn't ready for her to take off like that."

He laughs. "I can see that."

We turn and head into the house. Knox keeps Flower's leash in his hand instead of letting her off right away. "You can leave your shoes there, if you don't mind." He points to a rack with little shoes all lined up in a row. A few pairs that must be his also take up space. I slip off my shoes and add them to the shelf.

"Matti," Knox calls. He's managed to get Flower to sit beside him.

"Yay!" Matti squeals when he sees Flower sitting beside Knox. "Doggy!"

"Careful," Knox says, slowing Matti down with his voice. "We don't want to scare her. You have to be slow and gentle."

Matti moves closer to the dog, a smile plastered on his face. "Hold out your hand," Knox tells him.

Matti holds his little hand out and Flower leans in to sniff him. After a minute, Flower gives Matti a lick, eliciting a round of giggles from the small boy. "Pet!" Matti says excitedly. "I pet the dog?"

Knox nods. "Be gentle though."

I watch in awe as Flower sits perfectly still and lets Matti pet her. I'd never managed to get her to be so calm.

"All right," Knox says, patting Matti on the back. "Let's see if she can behave off her leash, shall we?"

Matti claps his hands, and I hold my breath. Knox unclips Flower and wraps the leash into a circle on the table in the foyer. Flower goes off to explore, sniffing this and that before finally settling on the plush rug in the center of the living room. Matti giggles and sits down next to her.

"Well, they seem to have hit it off," Knox says when Flower lays her head in Matti's lap.

"I guess so," I say. "I haven't seen her this gentle or calm before."

Knox glances at me and grins. "Maybe she just loves kids and didn't know what to do with herself without one around."

I watch as Flower gently licks Matti's hand. "You may be right."

Chapter Thirteen

Knox

AFTER MAKING SURE FLOWER and Matti are settled and getting along, I motion Lacey through to the kitchen. Thankfully the open concept of my sister's house lets me keep an eye on Matti no matter where I am in the main living space.

Lacey glances back at Matti and Flower cuddled together on the rug. "You know, I wonder if she has a family who's missing her."

I nod. "She just might. She does seem to have some manners already. And she's really good with Matti. Have you heard from the animal hospital yet?"

She sighs. "No, but I'll call tomorrow and see if they've managed to find anything."

"Well, I hope you like pizza," I say, changing the subject. "It's one of the things Matti seems to still like." I pull out the take-out boxes from the oven where I'd been keeping them warm.

"Sounds great!" Lacey takes the salad bowl from the counter and follows me to the dining area.

"Matti, it's time for dinner. Let's wash your hands," I call to him.

Matti jumps up from his place on the rug and runs to me. "Pizza time?"

I nod. "Yep, I got your favorite. Cheese."

He does a little dance and then grabs my hand, pulling me down the hallway to the bathroom.

I wait for everyone to be settled at the table with their food before striking up a conversation. "So, tell me about this center," I say to Lacey.

She finishes the bite in her mouth and takes a sip of water. "What do you want to know?"

"Where are you thinking of opening it? What kinds of things do you have in mind for programming and design? Your friend mentioned art and music and stuff ..."

She nods and wipes her hands on her napkin. "Well, ideally, I'd open it in the space next to the Coffee Loft. I see parents with their small kids there all the time."

I nod. "That would be a great space. Caffeine and kids' activities. Don't those go hand in hand?" I ask, raising an eyebrow. "I mean, I'm pretty sure I'm at least seventy-five percent caffeine nowadays."

Lacey laughs. "I imagine a lot of parents would agree with you."

"So, what kinds of things are you offering? Classes like story time at the library, or something else?"

"I'd like to have scheduled times that we would teach art, science, music, that sort of thing, but the center would be open from eight a.m. to three p.m. or so. There would be stations for free play. Comfortable seating so parents could take a break and still be near their kids. The space would be enclosed so that children couldn't run out the front door. It would be a safe, fun, educational environment for stay-at-home parents, or nannies and babysitters, to bring little ones under five during the day while their siblings are at school."

I take my time thinking about everything she's just shared. "That sounds amazing," I say finally. "I hope it happens for you." I really do. The passion in her eyes when she speaks about her center is consuming. It's clear this is what she's meant to do.

"Would it be a drop-off program?" I ask, mainly because if she opens the center, I would love for Matti to be a part of it.

She shakes her head. "No, I don't want to have to hire a huge staff. It wouldn't be a daycare, so I don't think it's necessary. A few parent volunteers to help out with running projects and keeping things clean is the goal. I figure I'll offer an hourly rate, an event rate, and a membership option. For parents who volunteer, I can discount their fees."

"That's really smart." I frown. "Does that mean I'll need to be looking for another nanny soon?"

She shakes her head. "If I'm lucky enough to open in the near future, I could just take Matti with me. If you sign a waiver, of course."

I grin. "I thought it wasn't a drop off?"

"It's not," she says. "But I can take Matti. He's my responsibility when I'm watching him, so that wouldn't change."

"That would be great," I say, relieved that I won't have to start this process over.

After dinner, Matti asks for the crayons and paper. We all sit down at the table and color together. It's nice. Relaxing in a strange way.

"I love your drawing, Matti. Can you tell me about it?" Lacey asks.

"Flower," Matti says, shrugging his shoulders.

Flower hasn't left Matti's side all evening. She lay beside him when he was eating, and is lying beside him now as he colors. He fidgets in his seat, and she stands, placing her head in his lap. He pets her and smiles.

My heart squeezes. "Hey, Lacey?"

She looks away from Matti and Flower and to me. "Yeah?"

"I can keep Flower here," I say. "Just until we know if she has a family." I'm not usually this impulsive, but seeing Matti so relaxed with Flower has melted me this evening.

"Are you sure?" she asks. "She's kind of a handful."

I nod. "You'll be here when I'm at work, and Matti seems to have bonded with her." I glance at them again. Flower's licking Matti's face, and he's smiling.

It feels right.

"Okay! I can run home and grab her crate for you." She pushes back her chair.

"That would be great," I say. "Thank you."

She stands and does the same happy dance Matti did when it was time for pizza. It's cute. "I'll be back soon," she says excitedly. She takes her keys and purse off the counter and heads for the front door.

"Let me walk you out," I say, standing.

"No, don't worry about it! I'll be back soon," she assures me.

Before I can get to the door, she is already across the lawn and climbing into her car. I smile and rub my hand over my heart. It's doing a weird thumping thing I've not experienced since high school when I had my first crush. Lacey is so much more than I first thought. She's kind and caring, thoughtful, energetic, and excited about her ideas. It's refreshing to spend time with a woman who is confident in who she is. *So much for not having a crush on the nanny.*

Giggles pull my attention back to the dining room where Matti and Flower are now cuddled together under the table. I rub my hand across my chest again. I'd do almost anything to hear more Matti giggles. Especially if it means keeping Lacey in our lives.

Chapter Fourteen

Lacey

MOM WAS RELIEVED WHEN I told her Knox and Matti offered to keep Flower—a feeling that redoubled after weeks went by and no one had claimed her. It's been several weeks since Flower became an official Sullivan family member. Knox had a trainer come work with her, and, since then, she's been a great member of the family, as well as a sweet companion for Matti.

I watch as Matti throws a ball across the backyard for Flower to chase.

"Matti," I call. "It's time to come inside." I gave Aurora my business plan to look over, and she asked if we can come in today to talk about it.

"Five minutes?" Matti asks.

I shake my head. "We can come play outside again when we get back. We're going to see Aurora today."

He runs to the porch, Flower close at his heels. "Rora!! Chocat milk!"

I laugh. Maybe we've been visiting the Coffee Loft too much. I shrug. I love coffee, and even though I tried, I can't get Knox's fancy coffee pot to work.

"Be a good girl," I say to Flower as I close her crate door. "No breaking out and destroying stuff."

Matti laughs. "Flower is a good girl."

I nod and pick him up. "I know, but just in case."

🐾 🐾 🐾 🐾 🐾

The bells above the door jingle when Matti and I walk into the Coffee Loft a few minutes later. There's a small line, so I take Matti to the corner booth to get settled. I've just pulled out his coloring book and box of crayons when Aurora slides into the booth across from me.

"Hey Matti," she says, holding up her hand for a fist bump.

"Rora!" Matti squeals and bumps his small fist to hers. "Chocat Milk?"

"It's coming," she says, pointing to Ashlan who has a chocolate milk and a coffee mug on her tray.

"Hi," she says, setting his milk in front of him, then setting mine down. "I made you a Raspberry White Chocolate Mocha."

I lean in and smell the coffee. "It smells so good. Thanks, Ash!"

"You're welcome." She grins and heads back to the counter.

"So," I say after taking a sip of the steaming hot coffee. "Did you have some suggestions to amp up my proposal?"

Aurora shifts in her seat. "Actually, I have a business proposition."

My mouth falls open. "What?" I ask, confused.

"I don't think you realized, but when I bought the coffee shop, I actually bought this building. I've been scouting the perfect business to put in the space next door."

I shake my head. Clearly I've started hearing things. "You what now?"

She laughs. "I bought the building. Well, actually my family did."

I take another sip of coffee and glance over at Matti, who is happily coloring in his coloring book.

"I don't think I understand what you're proposing."

She grins. "My family are real estate developers. When I saw the owner of the Coffee Loft was ready to retire, and the bookshop was moving locations, I talked it out with my parents, and we purchased the building and the Coffee Loft franchise."

"Okay," I say, taking it all in. "But what does that have to do with me?"

"I took a look at your proposal, and it's good. Really good. So I had a meeting with my family, and we'd like to back it."

"What?" I'm stunned. "What does that mean exactly?"

She passes over some papers for me to look at. "We'd like to give you a reduced rent for the space for the first year. We'd also like to open the two spaces up a bit. We thought having a half wall with a glass upper portion between the two spaces might help with marketing for both locations. A doorway in between for parents to slip over and order a coffee or a danish while their kids are at an event. That sort of thing."

She pauses while I flip through the papers.

"I think it's amazing!" I say finally. "But I don't have enough saved yet to purchase all the things we'd need to get started."

She nods. "I figured."

"So, what does that mean?" I'm trying hard to keep the walls in place and keep myself from getting too excited.

"It means that I can give you an advance on your salary to cover the expenses." Knox's deep voice causes me to jump in my seat, almost spilling my coffee.

I shake my head. "No, I don't feel comfortable with that."

He slides into the booth beside me. "Why not?"

"It's too much," I protest.

"Okay, then let me be an investor." He rubs his hands together and makes a funny face. "I know a good investment when I see one."

"Aren't you supposed to be at work?" I ask, raising a brow.

"I took the rest of the day off," he says, grinning. "When I stopped in for my morning coffee, Ashlan let it slip that Aurora was going to offer this. I couldn't miss it."

"This is a lot to take in, can I think about it?" I want to say yes right now, but this is a big decision.

"Of course," they both say.

"Take your time," Aurora says. "The space is yours if you want it."

She gets up to leave the table and Knox bumps my shoulder with his. Heat spreads through me at his touch. "What do you think?"

Think? How am I supposed to think when Knox is sitting so close to me with his leg touching mine under the table? How am I supposed to think when I might be able to open the center in months instead of years?

"Uh," I stammer. "I don't know. It's a lot to process."

"So, let's take the rest of the day and process." He reaches over me and squeezes Matti's hand. "Hey, Matti, how about we take Lacey on an adventure to Silver Dollar City this afternoon?"

Matti looks up, his little eyes as round as the saucers we serve danish on. "A dollar city?"

I laugh. "I can't possibly just go to Silver Dollar City today. That's crazy." I shake my head. "What about Flower?"

Knox takes my hands in his. "Seriously. Let's go have some fun. We can ride rides, watch the shows, and eat all the fun treats along the way. I gave Briella a house key. She's going to stop by and take care of Flower for me."

I take a deep breath, ready to tell him he and Matti should go when Matti climbs up onto the seat and wraps his arms around my shoulders.

"Pease!"

I laugh. Matti clearly already knows the buttons to push to get his way.

Knox leans in and squeezes my hand. "Please?"

"Oh, okay." I say. "Let's do it."

Chapter Fifteen

Knox

I GLANCE OVER TO the passenger seat where Lacey's staring out the window at the passing scenery. Taking the day off was a last-minute decision, but once I knew what Aurora was thinking, I couldn't help it. I wanted to be there for Lacey.

After spending the last few weeks getting to know her, I didn't want to miss being there when she learned she could make her dream a reality.

I glance over at her again. She's tapping her finger along with the music that plays softly while Matti naps in his car seat in the back. My heart stops for a second before beating a rhythm in my chest that I can't ignore.

I like her. A lot.

"So," I say, trying to reign in my wayward thoughts. "What are you thinking about over there?"

She blushes. Interesting.

"Nothing, really." She smiles sheepishly. "Okay, so everything."

I laugh. "Care to share?"

She takes a deep breath and shakes her head. "Not yet."

"Fair enough," I say. "Have you been to Silver Dollar City before?"

She nods. "It's been a while though."

"I've not been yet." I haven't been brave enough to leave Piney Brook with Matti. Maybe it's because I have Lacey with us that I feel confident doing it now. Or maybe I've finally settled into this new role.

Huh.

"You'll enjoy it. There's a lot to see and do. It's really fun." She grins. "Well, it was when I was here the last time."

I laugh. "I hear it's still great," I say, and wink at her. I can feel the blush form on my cheeks. I haven't winked at a woman in years. I've been too busy. I'd just started making time to date again when I found out about the accident. College and med school hadn't left me much time for a social life.

"Can I ask you something?" Lacey shifts in her seat to face me.

"Of course."

"Why did you move to Piney Brook when you became Matti's guardian?"

I shift uncomfortably in my seat. "Truth?"

She nods. "Always, please."

"The job I had in South Carolina was great. I loved it actually." I sigh. "When I found out about Sarah and Les ... well, it changed things for me. I didn't want to be obligated to such a high-stress position, working around the clock sometimes, when I had Matti to care for now."

Lacey leans over and places her hand on my shoulder, giving it a squeeze before dropping her hand back into her lap.

I smile at her before breaking eye contact. "Sarah and I were just out of high school when our mom passed away."

Lacey gasps. "I'm so sorry!"

I shrug. "It's okay. It's been a long time. We didn't know our dad. Well, I didn't anyway. Sarah remembered bits and pieces, but not much. I think that's why Sarah named me Matti's guardian in their will. She didn't want him to grow up without someone. Just in case."

Lacey wipes a tear from her eye. "What about Les's family?"

I shake my head. "Les grew up in foster care. They met when they attended the University of Arkansas. Les was a computer major, and Sarah was taking some classes to complement her business classes. He was too shy to ask her out at first, so he asked her to tutor him, even though he had straight A's. They hit it off, and got married right after graduation."

"That's so sweet," Lacey says, a soft smile on her lips.

"They were perfect for each other." I pause, fighting back the tears. "I never expected to lose them both, and I never thought I'd be a parent, honestly."

Lacey nods. "I get it. I don't see a family in the cards for me either."

I'm surprised at her admission. "Why not? You're beautiful, smart, young, driven, and so caring with kids. Why don't you see a family in your future?"

She laughs, a touch of bitterness making the sound false. "Three generations of failed marriages, single moms, and deadbeat dads—that's why."

I shake my head. "I don't follow."

She shoots me a sad look. "Not everyone is like you, Knox. My dad, my mom's dad, even her mom's dad ... they all left. Without a backward glance. There's something about the women in our family that make us unlovable."

I spot an exit up ahead, and slow the SUV, flipping on the blinker and maneuvering off the highway. I pull into the first gas station I see.

"Do you need the bathroom?" Lacey asks, unbuckling her seat belt.

"No," I say, searching her face as I consider my next words.

She turns and looks at me. "Okay, so, why did we stop, then?"

"You don't really think you're unlovable, do you?" I say softly, leaning towards her and brushing a strand of blue hair out of her face. She shivers. I fight back a smile. She may think she's unlovable, but I'm just as attracted to her as she is to me. At least, I hope she is.

"The evidence would point to that, yes."

"What evidence? A few deadbeats in your family tree?" I shake my head and place my hands on hers. "You are definitely lovable, Lacey Chambers."

She blushes, but I'm not finished.

"You make everyone around you feel like they're the most important person in the world. You stepped in and helped me, pretty much a total stranger, and I couldn't be more thankful. You deserve love, Lacey. You deserve happiness."

Her breath catches in her throat, and I fight the urge to lean in and press my lips against hers.

"I don't know what to say," she whispers.

"Say you'll keep an open mind. That you won't automatically rule out that good things can come your way." I rub my thumbs across the tops of her fingers, enjoying the way her skin feels against mine.

"Okay," she says finally. "I'll try."

I bring her hand to my lips and place a soft kiss. "That's all I can ask." Although I wanted to ask for more, I was afraid she wouldn't be open to it. Not yet.

She squirms in her seat. I let her hand go.

"Is it okay if I hop out and use the restroom now?" she asks.

I laugh. "Of course. Why didn't you say something?"

"You seemed pretty serious, and I didn't want to interrupt." She hops out of the car and turns, giving me a quick smile before closing the door softly so as to not wake the sleeping boy in the back seat.

I watch her run into the store and sigh. *How did she wiggle her way into my heart? When did I fall for the blue-haired beauty?*

Chapter Sixteen

Lacey

I RUSH INSIDE THE gas station and head directly for the restrooms. Thank goodness it's a one-stall situation. I lock the door behind me and pull my phone out of my back pocket. I dial and wait.

"Hello?" Bryce answers, panting like he's out of breath. "Everything okay?"

"No!" I screech. "Nothing is okay."

I hear some rustling and voices. "Okay, I'm stepping out of the training room. What's going on, Lace?"

I take a deep breath and glance in the mirror. My eyes are wide with panic. My cheeks are flushed, and my hair is wild since I just pulled it out of the ponytail and ran my hands through it.

"Spill it, Lace," Bryce says in his best dad voice. That's the thing about growing up without your dad around. Your big brother steps into the role of protector and best friend all at once.

"So, something kind of amazing may have happened. And then, we're going to Silver Dollar City and Knox says I'm lovable. I don't know. It's been a weird day. Now I'm hiding in a gas station bathroom calling you."

Bryce laughs. "Slow down. Take a breath. You're hiding in a bathroom? On the way to Silver Dollar City with who?"

"Knox. Didn't I say that already?" I circle my hand in the air as if that will help Bryce catch up.

"Your boss?" he asks. "You're going to a theme park with your boss who said you're lovable, and that was amazing?"

"That's not what I said! Keep up!" I rush. "No, Aurora and her parents own the building that the Coffee Loft is in. They offered me an amazing deal to help me start the education center right next door. I just don't have the start-up funds yet. So I don't know how that will work. Then, Knox comes in, sits next to me in the booth, offers to give me an advance on my nanny pay, and says we should take Matti to the theme park so I could get away and think it through."

I take a deep breath. "We were talking, and I told him about the curse. He said I'm lovable, but he doesn't understand."

"Wait!" Bryce says, halting my rambling. "Let's talk about the business opportunity when you're not hiding in the bathroom. I think I have an answer for you on that. Secondly, he's right. You *are* lovable. There's no curse, Lace. Just a string of bad guys. Not all guys are bad."

I scoff. "I know not all guys are bad. You're obviously not a bad guy, and Knox isn't either. What if it's me?"

Bryce sighs. "Lacey. It's not you any more than it was Mom, or Grandma. Sometimes things don't work out the way we plan.

Think of Matti. Do you think his parents thought they'd miss out on seeing him grow up?" He pauses. "No, they didn't. You can't control everything. Love is one of those things. Mom, Grandma, even our great-grandma loved the wrong man. That has nothing to do with you."

"But ..." I start.

"No, no buts. Now, I'm going back to my workout. You're going to get it together and enjoy your day."

"Okay," I say, taking a deep breath.

"Lacey?"

"Yeah?"

"It's okay to like him, you know. I'll call you tonight. I'm pretty sure I have the answer to your start-up issue. I just need to double check something first."

"I don't ... I mean ... How ...?"

"Bye, Lace."

Before I can get my thoughts together, Bryce has already hung up. I slip my phone into my pocket and splash some water onto my face. Looking at myself in the mirror, I take a deep breath and tell myself it's all going to be okay.

Talking to Bryce didn't solve any of my problems, but it did help me let go and focus on the now. Unfortunately, no one thought to check if Silver Dollar City is even open in early February. Spoiler alert, they aren't.

"I'm so sorry," Knox says, laughing. "I was so excited to come here with you guys today I didn't even think to look up if they were open."

I'm laughing so hard I'm crying. "This whole day has been wild," I say, wiping at the tears leaking from my eyes.

"Let's see what else there is to do in Branson in the middle of winter, shall we?"

I nod as Knox pulls out his phone.

"How about Branson's Wild World? Matti, you want to see some animals?" Knox asks, passing me his phone so I can see.

"Animals! Yay!" Matti yells from the back seat.

"Sounds good to me," I say, handing him back his phone.

Knox sets the GPS and pulls back out onto the highway. Thankfully it's just a fifteen minute detour to our new destination.

After securing tickets, we head inside the aquarium. Knox takes Matti from the stroller and holds him up so he can see the rays and sea turtles. We spend the afternoon leisurely walking through the exhibits and the outdoor animal enclosures, stopping each time something catches Matti's attention. After a while, he lays his head on Knox's shoulder and sighs.

"You okay, buddy?" Knox asks him, patting his back.

"I hungy."

"Ready to go and get some dinner?" Knox asks me.

I nod and turn the stroller around. I've been pushing it behind them as they stop at every animal's cage or tank to look. Watching Knox with Matti today has me questioning if maybe I've had it all wrong. Maybe the women in my family aren't cursed. Maybe the men they chose just weren't cut out for family life, like my brother said.

We stop at the gift shop on our way out where Matti picks out a sea turtle stuffie. "Mine," he says to the cashier as she tries to put it into a bag.

"What he means," Knox says, shooting a frown at Matti, "is that he'd like to hold it, please."

The cashier grins and hands it over to a waiting Matti. He holds the turtle tight with both hands and squeezes it to his chest. "Thank you," he says, not looking up from his new toy.

"You're welcome," the woman says, grinning. "You guys are a cute family." She hands Knox the receipt. "Have a great day."

Knox mumbles something that I can't quite make out and gives her a small wave.

I'm settling Matti into his seat while Knox puts the stroller back into the trunk.

"Yacey," Matti says. "I yuv you."

My breath catches in my throat and hot tears prick the backs of my eyes. "I love you, too, Matti." I lean in and give him a little kiss on the top of his head before closing his door and getting into the car.

Knox slides into the seat beside me and grins. "See. I told you you're lovable." He winks, and the gnomes get busy practicing their tap routine again.

"I'm starving," I say, ready to change the subject. "How about we get some dinner and head back?"

Knox nods and buckles his seatbelt. "You got it. I think I saw a steakhouse around the corner. Does that sound good?"

"Sure," I say, clipping my seat belt into place. "Sounds great."

Chapter Seventeen

Knox

THE STEAKHOUSE IS RUSTIC. Animal horns hang on dimly-lit walls. Our seating options are wooden tables and brown vinyl booths on the perimeter, or square tables and wooden chairs in the center of the room. The rich aroma of sizzling meat hangs in the air.

"Party of three?" the hostess asks.

"Please, and a high chair if you have one," Lacey answers.

She nods and gathers menus and rolls of silverware. "Right this way."

Thankfully, she leads us to a booth in the back corner.

"This okay?" she asks, laying the menus on the table.

"Perfect," I say, holding Matti in my arms.

Lacey slides into the booth across from me and takes off her jacket. Her blue hair hangs over her shoulders today, and the turquoise of her sweater brings out the blue-green in her eyes. "Smells good in here," she says, picking up her menu.

"It does," I agree. The hostess brings a high chair, and I get busy settling Matthias in and taking his jacket off. "Are you ready to eat?" I ask him.

"Hungy," he says, nodding his head. "Chicken, please."

I smile and point to the kids' menu. "You bet." I'm so thrilled he's starting to speak more. It's been a rough few months, but I think we are turning a corner.

After we place our orders—a steak for me, grilled chicken for Lacey, and chicken tenders for Matti—I settle back in the booth and watch Matti giggle as he and Lacey color the kids' menu they put in front of him when we were seated.

A warm feeling of contentment washes over me. I could get used to days like this. I smile as Lacey looks up and grins at me.

🐢　🐢　🐢　🐢　🐢

By the time we pull into the driveway, it's late. Matti is asleep in his seat, cuddling his stuffed turtle tightly.

"I'll go open the door and turn on some lights, and let Flower out while you bring Matti inside so she doesn't wake him up." Lacey slips out of the SUV and gently closes the door.

I watch as she makes her way up the sidewalk and opens the door. Teamwork really does make parenting easier.

Carefully, I unbuckle Matti from his seat. I smile when I see his shoes on the seat beside him. At least he's left his socks on. It's cold tonight.

Lacey and Flower are outside the back sliding glass door when I step into the house and toe my shoes off. I pause for a moment and watch them. It seems so natural to have Lacey here. A part of things.

After settling Matti in his bed, I pull his bedroom door almost closed, leaving it cracked open in case he needs me. I hear Lacey filling Flower's food and water dishes in the kitchen and head back down the hallway to help.

"You don't have to do that," I say as I reach the kitchen.

"I know, but you were laying Matti down. It's no problem."

This. This is why I was never interested in seriously dating before. The women I would go out with were only concerned with themselves. Lacey is extraordinarily caring and giving. So different from any other women I've had feelings for.

Whoa, I think to myself. *I have feelings for her. Real ones.* "Hey, Lacey? Do you need to get home right away, or would you like some hot chocolate? Extra whipped cream," I say, hoping to entice her.

"Well, if you're offering extra whipped cream, how could I refuse?" she asks, chuckling as she gives Flower a rubdown.

I grin and get to work making two hot chocolates with extra whipped cream. "Want to take these to the living room?"

"Sure," she says, standing. I follow her and her steaming mug to the couch.

"Have you given any more thought to Aurora's proposal?" I ask.

She nods. "I talked to my brother about it for a few minutes earlier today. He said he might have a way to help me get funded." She pulls out her phone and frowns. "He said he'd call me back tonight, but I haven't heard from him yet." She sets the phone on the coffee table and slips her feet underneath her legs.

"How old is your brother?" I ask, realizing we haven't talked much about her family besides the so-called curse.

"He's twenty-six. Two years older than I am, but he's always been my best friend." She sighs and takes a sip of her hot drink. "I don't see him as much as I'd like to these days, but that's what happens when you have a professional hockey player for a brother, I suppose."

I choke on my drink. "What did you say your brother's name was?" I ask when I finally stop sputtering.

"Bryce. Bryce Chambers. He plays for the D—"

"Denver Edge," I finish. "Wow, I didn't realize Bryce was your brother."

"You follow hockey?" she asks, grinning. "I had you pegged for a football guy."

I shrug. "You're not technically wrong. These days I'm watching all the sports."

"Huh?"

"Well, as you can tell by Matti's room, Les was a big Ozark Legends fan. He was always talking about taking Matti to games and playing catch with him when he got a little bigger." I stop and take a deep breath. "So I'm trying to learn the sport. I'm watching reruns of this past season's games, hoping to figure out who the players are and what the rules are. Besides the obvious ones everyone knows, that is."

Lacey puts her drink down on the coffee table and puts her hand on my knee. My leg tingles in the best way. "That's so sweet of you."

Her hand is burning through the denim of my jeans. It's like I can feel it directly on my skin. "Lacey," I say, more gruff than I intended. "You have a little ..." I point to her mouth where a bit of cream has stuck to her lip. I slowly reach out a hand and wipe the cream from her mouth with my thumb. Her breath hitches, and her cheeks turn a lovely pink. "Got it," I whisper, my mouth inching closer to hers.

I wait for her to back away, to put a stop to this ... but she doesn't. Her eyes drift closed, and she leans slightly forward. Gently, I brush my lips across hers before pulling back and waiting for her to look at me.

When her eyes open, sparkling pools of blue-green stare back at me. "Lacey, I like you. A lot."

She brings her hand to her mouth and gently touches her lips. "What about the curse? I don't want to hurt you. Or Matti."

I shake my head. "I don't believe there is a curse. Even if there were, no one can predict the future. All we have is now. Our time together here."

She nods.

"Do you ... do you think you may like me too?" I ask, hesitating to make myself totally vulnerable.

She looks away, and my heart sinks in my chest. "It's okay if you don't," I say, trying to keep the hurt out of my voice.

Lacey stands and walks to the front windows. She clasps her hands together and takes her time looking out into the night before she turns and gives me a soft smile. "I think I've had feelings for you since the day you spilled hot coffee all over yourself in the Coffee Loft."

My chest feels like it's just been cracked open for heart surgery. "You have?"

She nods. "I have."

I stand and join her at the window. "What now?" I ask, taking her hands in mine.

She leans her head on my shoulder and sighs. "I have no idea."

Chapter Eighteen

Lacey

"*WHAT NOW*" *INDEED.* I've spent my whole life thinking I could outrun my feelings. That they were something I could control, and here I am. Eyebrows-deep in them. Ugh!

"I think I should get home," I say, even though I'm not quite ready to let go of Knox. "It's getting late."

He nods, but doesn't let me go. "Okay."

After a few more minutes in his arms, I pull away. "I'll see you in a few days." I work at the Coffee Loft tomorrow, and he's off the day after.

Knox clears his throat. "Would it be too much if I gave you a goodbye kiss?"

I pretend to think about it before bursting out in a fit of giggles. I'd love for him to kiss me again. He stands by while I slide my shoes and jacket back on before he opens the door for me to step through.

"I'll walk you to your car," he says, reaching for my hand.

"What about Matti?" I ask. "What if he wakes up and needs you?"

He frowns. "I didn't think of that."

I reach up and place my arms around his neck. "Just kiss me here," I whisper.

And he does.

So thoroughly, in fact, that I'm still thinking about it when I step inside my house.

"There she is," Mom says from her spot on the couch. "I've been waiting for you."

I slip off my shoes and hang my jacket on the hook. "You have?" Sure, we live together, but it's not like she waits up for me anymore. Well, not usually, anyway.

"I have. Can we talk?" She pats the couch next to her.

"Uhm, sure?" I have a seat and turn toward her. "This is starting to weird me out. What's going on?"

"Bryce called me." She says, rubbing her hands on her pants. "He told me something pretty interesting. A few things, actually."

"That bugger!" I say. "He's supposed to be a vault."

Mom laughs and shakes her head. "Just listen," she says, her laughter fading.

I nod. "Okay, you have my attention."

Mom takes a deep breath. And then another. "The thing is, Bryce mentioned you think we're cursed."

I fan my face. "Did you turn the heat up too high tonight? I haven't been home ten minutes and I'm sweating."

"You're fine," Mom says. "Can you stay focused, please?"

"Uh, sure. Cursed." I pull my hair off my neck and knot it in a messy bun.

"We aren't cursed, Lacey, though I guess I could see why you might think that. The women in this family aren't so great about discussing our feelings." She shrugs. "What can I say?"

I stare at her a moment, waiting for her to finish this line of thought, but she doesn't. She just stares off into the distance like she can see something I can't. "Mom ..." I prod.

"Oh, right. Your great-grandfather was a good man. He didn't leave your Grandma May because he wanted to. He left to find work in the oil fields, except there was an accident and he didn't make it home." She wipes a tear from her eye. "Grandma May never talked about it again. I think her heart was broken until the day she passed."

"Oh," I whisper, rubbing the ache that has started in my chest. "Poor Grandma May."

"That's not all," Mom says. "My dad. Well, he was a different story." She shudders. "We don't talk about it because it was a bad time. He had a drinking problem. When he would drink, he'd get mean. One day, he left, and just never came back. We were all relieved, honestly."

I lean in and give Mom a hug. "I had no idea. I'm so sorry."

She shakes her head. "That's all in the past. He didn't drink like that when Grandma first married him. It started after he lost his job. He couldn't provide for his family, and by then they'd had all five of us kids. That did something to him, and he couldn't undo it."

I wrap my arms around my middle. "Okay, and my dad?" I ask, hoping there's a better explanation than the one I've been dreaming up my whole life. The one where he decided my mom, Bryce, and I were too much.

"That's what I brought you here to talk about." She nods toward the hallway, and I turn to see what she's gesturing at.

"Your dad was dumb and made a huge mistake," a man says, stepping around the corner. "Your mom and I ... we were young and didn't know what else to do at the time. I should have fought harder to stay in your lives."

"What in the hot potato is happening?" I ask, jumping from the couch.

"I called your father, and explained how you felt," Mom says, standing and walking to his side. "He wanted to come and tell you his side in person."

I shake my head. "No. No way. What? No."

The man—my dad, I guess—holds his hands up in front of him. "I know you're mad at me. I don't blame you. I've been mad about this for more than two decades."

"Fine," I say, holding myself tight. "Shouldn't Bryce be here?"

"We're talking to him later. I've already asked him to face time with me later. We didn't want you to have to wait."

I suck in a breath and push it out, then turn to Dad and say, "Well, go ahead."

Dad smiles and I see that Bryce has his mouth and eyes. It makes my dad seem familiar even though I don't remember ever seeing him before. "It's a long story, and one I wish had ended differently." He sits down on the couch cushion which Mom just vacated. "My parents were wealthy. Very wealthy. And very controlling."

I glance at Mom who nods and sits in the chair on the other side of the room. I can't bring myself to sit back down, so I stand, my arms wrapped around my middle.

"Your mom was the daughter of the beautiful woman who came to clean our house. Sometimes your mom would come with her, and we'd sneak away and get to know each other. She was the only girl I knew who didn't look at me like I was her ticket to an easy life. We fell deeply in love and couldn't get enough of each other."

He turns and smiles at my mom. "Anyway, we got ahead of ourselves and your brother was born. My parents were furious when we told them we were having a baby, and that we wanted to get married. They demanded we give him up for adoption, but we just couldn't do it."

Mom wipes a tear from her eye. "They were very persistent. Went out of their way to make my life, and your father's life, difficult. They were powerful in the community, and had friends in high places, as they say. When Bryce was just weeks old, they sued for custody, dragging me through the mud in the process. They had money for cutthroat lawyers, and the judge was in their pocket. I had nothing."

He nods his head and continues. "They said they'd back off and let your mom be if I stayed away from her. They didn't want it to get out that their heir had an illegitimate child."

I frown. "And you agreed to this?" I ask my mom.

"I did. It was either that or lose your brother. It was the only way we could see forward at the time. We even left town during the trial to get away from them, but the police found us in the motel, and took Bryce away. I hate thinking of that night. We fought to get away, but they pried him out of my arms and locked us in jail. His parents sent their lawyers, who told us if we would sign an agreement, they'd leave us alone. I was frantic to sign—I didn't know if I'd ever see Bryce again unless I did. Your father didn't want to bow to their demands, but he did, for my sake."

I turn back to my father. "So then, if you agreed to stay away, how am I here?"

He looks to my mom, who gives him a slight nod. "When Bryce was a baby, I used to sneak away and visit your mom. I'd say I was going away on business, and spend time with them. I loved them both so much, and it tore me apart to stay away."

I shake my head. "So, I was another mistake?"

My mom gasps, and leaps from her spot on the chair, coming to stand next to me, and takes my hands in hers. "No, no way. You and your brother are the best things that have ever happened to me."

I stare at her, dumbfounded. "Really? Is that why you cried at night? Why you sometimes worked two jobs to make ends meet?"

Mom sits down on the couch, still holding my hand, and pats the seat next to her, between her and Dad. "I know it's a lot to take in, but that's how it had to be. I didn't regret you two. Ever. I missed your dad, and hated spending so much time away from you for work, but I never regretted you."

I glare at my father. "And if your family had any sense, or any hearts, they wouldn't have let her struggle with two small children." My hands ball into fists at my side.

"You're right," Dad says. "Absolutely right. The problem is they didn't have sense. They had an agenda. I sent your mom money every chance I got for years. Then my parents caught wind of it and started up their harassment again. They weren't good people. Eventually, your mom asked me to just keep my distance, to stop all contact. She broke up with me so we could both live our lives in peace. It wasn't an easy choice, but it seemed like the only way at the time."

I raise an eyebrow at that. "You said your parents 'weren't' good people? As in, they are no longer here?"

Dad nods. "They passed away a few years ago now. The first thing I did after my mother took her last breath was call Ellen."

"Uh huh," I say, glancing at Mom. "And you've been talking to her since then?"

He nods.

"But not me and Bryce?" I feel the tears spill over my cheeks and wipe them furiously away. "Why not?"

My mom pulls me into her arms. "That's my fault," she says. "I didn't know how you and your brother would react to finding out the truth. It was easier to keep the status quo than to explain. I'm sorry. I'm so sorry."

I glance between my parents. "Did you ever marry?" I ask my dad.

He shakes his head slowly and glances at my mom. "No, I'd already found my one true love, but I didn't believe I could have her."

Mom turns to him, her own tears making her mascara run. *At least we'll look like racoons together,* I think to myself.

I nod. "I think I understand, or I'm trying to, at least."

"There's more," Dad says, reaching across for Mom's hand, which she gives him. "This time it's good news, or at least, I hope it is."

Chapter Nineteen

Knox

THERE'S A LOUD BANGING noise at the park where Matti and I are tossing a ball back and forth. "Do you hear that?" I ask him, but he just throws the ball back to me. I turn to find the noise, and fall directly out of the bed.

It was a dream. I rub my backside. There's a hint of morning sun streaming through the small crack in the curtains. I rub my eyes. I could have sworn ... The banging at the door starts again.

"Coming," I shout. I race down the hallway, tugging my shirt on over my head. When I turn the corner into the living room, my socked feet slide out from under me, bringing me crashing down and colliding into the end table beside the couch. Thankfully, it's empty and nothing falls and breaks. *Toddler proofing for the win,* I think as I stand back up. There's got to be a limit to how many times a guy can fall on his derriere in one day, right?

I look through the peephole, and panic. I swing the door open and barely step out of the way as Lacey comes barging into the room.

"Did you know there's no curse?" she asks, her hands on her hips. She strides past me and starts pacing from the door to the coffee table and back as she speaks. "Just a crazy line of weird stories." She shakes her head. "All this time, I thought my dad didn't love me."

I stand there, rubbing my bruised backside, and trying to figure out what she's talking about. One thing I've learned about Lacey is that she often starts in the middle of a story, but she'll bring it back around if you give her enough time.

"I didn't think there was a curse," I say gently, hoping it's the right thing to say.

"Well, you were right," she says, throwing me a small grin.

Phew!

"Good, I'm glad," I say, smiling at the warmth she's showing me.

"Where's Flower?" she asks.

"I moved her crate into the laundry room at night. She seems to do better away from the main part of the house, where she hears every little noise." I move to the couch and sit down.

"Oh, that's smart," she says. "I didn't wake Matti up, did I?"

I shake my head. "I don't think so. How long were you out there knocking?"

She looks at her phone and back at me. "I don't know. A few minutes, maybe."

"Why didn't you just use the key?" I ask.

Her eyebrows disappear under her blue bangs. "And scare you this early in the morning? No thanks."

I stifle a laugh. As if her banging on the door hadn't scared the living daylights out of me. "Makes sense," I finally manage to say.

She nods.

"Care to start at the beginning?" I ask, motioning for her to join me on the couch.

She sits and crosses her ankles. "I met my dad last night."

"Whoa!" I say, letting out a big breath. "Were you expecting that?"

She shakes her head no. "Apparently Bryce called my mom and told her about our conversation. She and my dad have been talking for a few years now."

I rub my hands over my face. "Okay ..."

"But not me and Bryce," she says, frowning. "Because my mom thought she was protecting us or something. So anyway, there's no curse. Just a bunch of people who made poor choices. Can you believe it? Well, except my great-grandpa. He couldn't have known he'd get in that accident."

I place my hand on her knee, and she takes a steadying breath. "I'm glad there's no curse." I say, smiling. "Does that mean you believe you're lovable now?"

She looks at me for a minute before nodding slightly. "I think I believed that before I left here last night."

Warmth spreads through my chest and out to my limbs. "That is the best news I've heard all morning."

"Well, just you wait, because there's more." She grins. "Apparently, my mean old grandparents were rich. And now they're gone, so my dad is rich. Do you know what that means?"

I shake my head. "Not really, no."

"It means that I can have my inheritance early. Well, part of it anyway. Enough to give me the start-up funds I need to open the center!"

She claps her hands in front of her. "And, I get a dad. It doesn't make up for the last twenty-four years, but it's something right? Besides, get this ... he never stopped loving my mom. I don't think she stopped loving him either because she never even dated when I was growing up." She wiggles her eyebrows up and down. "Maybe I'll have a real family."

She throws herself into me for a hug. "Maybe I'll even have a family of my own one day." She whispers it into my t-shirt, but I hear it, and I can't stop the grin that tugs on my lips.

I hold her close and breathe in her scent. Vanilla and sugar. She always smells like the best fresh-baked cookies.

"Don't you need to go to work today?" I ask, eyeing her Coffee Loft apron.

She nods. "Yes, but I needed to come tell you that I think I know what's next."

"You do?" I ask, forcing the words past my heart that is now sitting in my throat.

She leans in and places her lips on mine. A soft kiss that means so much.

"I do."

"What's next?" I ask, holding my breath.

Chapter Twenty

Lacey

I PLACE BOTH HANDS on Knox's cheeks and look him right in his eyes. "We give this a chance. I don't want to wait twenty-four years to tell you how I feel. I want to tell you now."

He nods, but waits for me to continue.

"I'm falling for you, Knox Sullivan. You're the kindest, most caring man I've ever known. I see you with Matti, and all the love you have for him, and I can imagine that same love pouring out for your own children one day. I'm not saying I know what the future holds, but I am saying I'd like us to find out together."

Knox opens his mouth to speak, but I place a finger over his lips. "Not now. I have to go to work, but do you think we could talk later? My mom offered to watch Matti if you think that's okay."

"She did?" he asks.

"She did," I say, nodding. "When I told her how I felt about you, she jumped at the chance to get to know him better."

Knox grins. "I think that would be great."

"She won't watch Flower, though. Seems she doesn't believe she's a reformed pooch."

Knox laughs and holds me tight. "I'd love to meet your mom, too, and introduce her to Matthias. Is that okay?"

"Of course," I say. "In fact, I was going to invite you both to dinner at my house tonight to meet her. Next weekend Bryce will be in town to play the Little Rock Rockies, so my dad wants to have dinner with the whole family on Sunday. I'd love for you to come then too, and meet my brother and my dad."

"I don't know," Knox says hesitantly. "Isn't that a family thing?"

I sigh. "I think my boyfriend and his son qualify."

He grins and pulls me in for another sweet kiss. "Is that what I am?" he asks.

I shrug. "I'd like for you to be. If that's what you want, too."

"Uncle Knox!" Matti calls, running down the hallway. "Uncle Knox!"

"In here, buddy," Knox calls out, getting up to go to him.

Matti turns the corner with tears in his eyes. "You're not in bed."

"I'm sorry," I say gently. "I came over and woke Uncle Knox up too early."

Matti notices me for the first time and smiles. "Yacey!"

"Hey, Matti," I say, standing and ruffling his hair. "I've got to go to work, but I'll see you soon, okay?"

He nods and reaches out to Knox who lifts him up and holds him tight. "I'm sorry you were scared," he whispers as he leans in to place a gentle kiss on Matti's cheek.

"S'okay," Matti says, wrapping his arms around Knox's neck and holding tight. "I hungy."

I lean in and give both of my guys a peck on the cheek. "I'll see you guys later."

* * * * *

The Coffee Loft is eerily quiet when I step through the front door. "Hello?" I call out. The front door was unlocked, so I know someone has already come in for the day. I move toward the swinging door that separates the front from the storage and office area. "Hello?" I call again.

"Hey!" Aurora says, poking her head out the office door. "Sorry, I was just putting some things away."

"No worries, I just didn't know who was here. It's kind of creepy to open the door to no one." I laugh and place my hand on my chest.

Aurora grins. "Have you given any more thought to my proposal?" she asks.

"Not wasting any time I see." I bust out laughing. "I have, and ... we have a deal."

She squeals and grabs my hands before jumping up and down. "I think this is going to be perfect!" she says between jumps. "Plus, you'll be right next door, so it's like you never left!"

"Is it bad that I'm nervous?" I ask. "Everything is happening so fast. It's like everything I ever wished for is coming true at the same time."

She grins. "I can see why that might feel overwhelming. In a good way, I hope?"

"In the best way," I say as the door chimes and in walk Knox and Matti holding hands. "The very best way."

Knox steps up to the counter. "Are we too early?" he asks, waving to Aurora.

"Not at all," I say, starting the coffee pot and turning on the register. "What can I get you today?"

"The usual," Knox says, looking over at Matti. "I'm afraid to try anything new."

I meet his eyes. "Sometimes the best things come from trying something new."

He smiles and moves over to the case of pastry. "What looks good today, Matthias?"

Matti takes his time looking at each option before pointing out the blueberry scone. "Dat one."

Knox and I both laugh. "Then again, there's something to be said for going after your favorites," Knox says with a wink. "Speaking of going after things. I was wondering if you'd be my date to the hospital's Valentine charity ball this weekend."

Aurora bumps me with her hip. "She'd love to."

"Hey," I say, laughing. "I can answer for myself!" I turn to Knox and wink. "I'd love to."

"Think your mom could watch this little guy?" he asks.

"I think she'd love too," Mom says from behind Knox. She squats down next to my favorite three-year-old and smiles at him. "Hey, there. Matti, right?"

"When did you come in?" I ask. "We really need to get the chimes on the door fixed, Aurora."

She laughs and nods. "I'll call maintenance today."

"I came in just in time to hear this handsome young man ask you to be his Valentine, and I heard you accept." She reaches out her hand for Knox to shake. "You must be the guy who has my daughter's heart. It's a pleasure to meet you."

"Mom!" I squeal. "It's too soon for all of that," I whisper loud enough for everyone to hear.

Knox winks at me. "I don't know if I have her heart quite yet, but I know she's got mine."

Epilogue

One Year Later

Knox

I PULL THE CRIMSON tie into a full Windsor knot and walk to the floor-length mirror to make sure it's in the right place. Turning to the side a half-step, I take in my reflection. Tonight's the annual Piney Brook General charity gala, and officially one-year since Lacey and I became a couple.

I run my fingers through my hair to make sure it looks like it did when I left Masters Cuts and More this morning. Anne, the head stylist, was able to slip me in for a quick cleanup. She didn't mind staying late for me after I told her what's in store for tonight.

"Uncle Knox," Matti yells down the hallway. "Grandma's here!"

I grin and take one last look in the mirror. Matthias has really bonded with Lacey's mom over the last year.

"Coming," I call back. I grab my wallet and keys from their place on the nightstand and step into the hallway.

"Sprinkles, too?" I hear Matti ask.

"Of course," Ellen says, clapping her hands together. "You can't make celebration cupcakes without sprinkles!"

"What are we cel-a-brating?" Matti asks, slowly pronouncing the big word.

"Well ..."

"We're celebrating Valentine's Day. Right, Grandma?"

Ellen rushes to me and throws her arms around my middle. "I'm just so excited!"

I hug her back. "Let's not get ahead of ourselves. I haven't even mentioned it to Lacey yet."

She nods. "I know! She has no idea. It's going to be so amazing!"

I laugh. "I hope she agrees with you."

I step around to where Matti's sitting on top of the counter surrounded by enough frosting and sprinkles to supply a bakery. "Be good for Grandma, okay?" I lean in and kiss his head.

"I will!" He leans his head on my chest for a moment before pulling back and looking up at me. "You be good, too. Kay?"

I cross my fingers over my heart. "Promise."

"You better get going," Ellen says, shooing me toward the front door with a dish towel. "You can't be late."

"Okay, Mom," I say, mostly joking.

She beams and opens the front door. "Good luck!"

I step onto the front porch into the cold night air. "Thanks."

Twenty minutes later, I'm standing on Lacey's front porch. I ring the doorbell and wait, nerves making my hands shake slightly.

The door swings open, and my jaw falls to the floor. "You look beautiful," I say when I finally find my brain again. "Wow."

Lacey spins in a little circle. "You think so? It's not too much?" She fluffs her short brown hair. The deep emerald green of the strapless dress she's wearing hugs her perfectly, and complements the red tie and pocket square I've chosen.

"When did you ..."

"I wanted to surprise you," she says. "I made an after-hours appointment with Anne last night."

I smile and pull her to me for a hug. "I hope you know you didn't have to do that. I love your wild hair colors." She's had blue, red, pink, and even gray hair over the last year, and I've loved every version of her she's shown me.

She leans back and searches my eyes. "You don't think you deserve a 'normal' girlfriend?"

"Lacey, I hope I always deserve you. In all of your wonderful shades." I kiss her wrinkled forehead. "You're beautiful no matter what color your hair is."

She leans in and presses her lips gently to mine. "Thank you," she whispers.

"You look stunning. That dress looks like it was made for you," I say, letting her step away from me.

She blushes. "Thank you. I'd hope it isn't too much. I know it's more of a Christmas color than Valentine's, but I just love it."

"It's perfect, just like you. Are you ready to go?" I glance at my watch. "We have a few more minutes if you need more time."

She shakes her head and grabs her bag and a matching green wrap from the back of the couch. "I'm ready if you are."

The community center lobby is decorated with soft pink lights, huge white hearts, and Cupid's bows everywhere. "It looks like we stepped into a Valentine's Day card," Lacey says as we wait in line to enter the main event room.

I laugh. "You're not wrong." I take her hand and slide it through my arm. "I'm so glad you are my date tonight," I whisper so only she can hear me.

She lays her head on my shoulder. "Me too."

Once inside the event room, round tables take up most of the space with a small area in the center set up to be a dance floor. Red tablecloths and vases of white roses adorn each table.

"Wow," Lacey says as we make our way to our table near the dance floor. "They definitely upped the budget this year."

I laugh. "It appears that way." I wave at Briella who's just walked in with her friend Reid. "Want to go say hi?"

Lacey turns to look where I'm pointing. "Sure!"

We weave our way through the tables to where Briella and Reid are standing near the silent-auction tables. "Hello," I say as we approach.

"Hey! You clean up nice," Briella says, looking me up and down. "And you're stunning as usual," she says to Lacey, leaning in for air kisses. "You remember my friend, Reid?"

Reid and I shake hands. "I do. Nice to see you here."

He smiles and looks at Briella. "I'm happy to be here to keep her company tonight."

Lacey squeezes my hand and quickly tips her head toward the two of them. I squeeze back. I see it too. Reid is looking at her like she's the only one in the room.

"Well, we're going to find our seats," Briella says. "We'll see you." She takes Reid's hand and guides him across the room to a table with some other nurses from the hospital.

I recognize Mona from the hospital, and wave. "Let's look at the silent-auction options."

Hand in hand we walk the row of offerings. A family pack of season passes to Silver Dollar City catches my attention. "We should try to go back, when they're open this time."

Lacey laughs. "That would be fun. I bet Matti would love it."

I pick up the pen and write my bid on the auction form. It's well more than the passes cost, but it's for a good cause. The hospital holds the gala each year to raise funds for a scholarship they offer to patients who wouldn't be able to afford care otherwise.

Lacey wanders farther down the table and stops. I step up beside her to see what caught her eye. I grin when I see the brochure for Matti's Playhouse. "Looks like people are interested in winning a membership to your center."

She turns to me and grins. "Did you put this up for auction?"

I nod. "I thought it might be a hit."

"Thank you," she says, leaning in and kissing me softly. "It means so much to me that you support my dreams."

I pull her close and lean in. "You, and Matti, are my dream."

I release her as they announce it's time to make our way back to the tables.

I glance around the room until I spot Briella. She gives me a slight nod, and I mouth, "Thank you." I think I might throw up. I'm so

nervous. I glance around the room. Maybe this isn't the right time
...

"What's that?" Lacey asks as she steps closer to our table. "Knox, there's something on my plate." She looks around at the rest of the plates in the room. "What in the world?"

I pull out her seat for her, and she sits and plucks the box from the plate. "It's got my name on it."

"Open it," I say, pulling my chair back.

She carefully pulls the lid of the box up, revealing a sparkling diamond engagement ring nestled in the soft velvet lining. "Knox!" She gasps and turns to look at me.

I sink down onto one knee. "Lacey Chambers, you have made me the happiest man in the world. Matti and I would love it if you would consider joining our family."

Lacey's eyes begin to water, and I gently take the box from her hand. "I love your kind spirit, your sense of humor, the way you love those around you. I love your excitement over little things, and your adventurous hairstyles. I love you, Lacey Chambers. Will you be my wife?"

The room is so quiet, you could hear a pin drop. Butterflies violently float about in my chest.

Lacey wipes her eyes and smiles the most radiant smile I've ever seen. "Yes!"

I stand and pull her up into my arms. "She said yes!" I shout for all to hear.

The room erupts in cheers as I press my lips to Lacey's, but all hear is my heartbeat settling into place.

✿ ✿ ✿ ✿ ✿

Lacey

I glance at the ring Knox slid onto my finger just a few hours ago, and smile. A year ago, I never would have guessed this would be my life.

"Do you mind if we make a quick stop before I drop you off at home?" Knox asks.

"Of course not." I sit back into the cozy heated leather seats. "I can't believe we are engaged!"

Knox takes my hand in his. "I'm the luckiest guy on earth."

I feel like I'm floating on a cloud like they do in cartoons. If I can find my happily-ever-after, anything's possible. I laugh out loud at that thought.

"What's so funny?" Knox asks, giving my fingers a light squeeze.

"I was just wondering if you could see little hearts floating above my head." I shake my head and chuckle again. "It's weird, I know. I just never expected to fall in love and have my own family. Now ..." I pause and gather my thoughts. "Now, I'm getting the whole shebang, and I feel like it's a dream, truly."

Knox smiles at me. "If it's a dream, I don't want us to wake up. Deal?"

"Deal," I say.

He pulls the car into a parking space and shuts off the engine.

"What are we doing here?" I ask, confused. Gabby is waving at us from the front doors of Beats and Eats where I can see people inside.

"Don't be upset, please?" Knox asks, looking a tiny bit worried.

"Upset about what?" I draw. "What did you do, Knox Sullivan?"

"Are y'all getting out or what? Gabby's letting in a draft," a voice I'd know anywhere calls from outside.

"Bryce!" I squeal, opening the door and running to my brother. "I didn't think I'd see you for another few months," I say, jumping into his arms and giving him a huge bear hug.

He laughs and sets me down on my feet. "Well, your future husband had other plans." He points to where Knox is closing the door I left wide open in my excitement.

"You got my brother to come to town in the middle of the season?" I ask, surprise lacing my voice.

Knox nods.

"Come on, then," Bryce says, moving out of the doorway. "No sense standing out in the cold."

Gabby grins and holds the door open for Knox and me to walk through. "Congratulations," she whispers as I pass her.

"Thanks," I say as I step inside the doorway.

"Yacey!" Matti yells, causing me to whip my head around. Beats and Eats is packed! Friends and family fill the diner.

"Well," Mom says, coming up to Knox and me. "How'd it go?"

My dad steps in and gives me a side hug. While I wish he'd been around when I was younger, we've been working on getting to know each other over the last year. He really is a good guy.

Knox holds up my hand and she squeals so loudly Matti throws both hands over his ears.

"Congrats, sweetheart," Dad says, kissing my temple. "You two are a great fit."

"Jeez, Grandma, not so youd!"

Knox chuckles. For as much progress as Matti has made with his speech, he still struggles with the 'l' sound. "Grandma's just excited, bud."

"About what? Yacey's pretty ring?"

Knox kneels down to his level. "Remember when I asked you how you'd feel if Lacey became part of our family?"

Matti nods. "My aunt."

"Yes. Well, I asked Lacey if she would be my wife, your aunt, tonight," Knox says, looking up at me and smiling sweetly.

"Well?" Matti demands, stomping his little foot and turning to face me. "What did you say?"

I scoop him into my arms, careful not to rip my dress. "I said yes. I'm so glad you want me to be a part of your family." I hug him tight. "I love you, Matthias."

"Can we have the cupcakes now?" He wiggles in my arms until I let him down. "Grandma helped me make them!"

"Time for cupcakes," Knox announces, following Matti to the table where a few dozen cupcakes with pink frosting and little heart-shaped sprinkles are set out in the shape of a heart.

Matti hands us each a cupcake, and points to a table that's been moved to the middle of the room. "You're 'posed to sit there," he says, pushing us gently from behind.

Knox and I take our seats, laughing.

"Congratulations to the happy couple," Briella says, stepping up to the table.

"Yes," Reid says from behind her. "We should all be so lucky some day." He looks at Briella and grins.

As they move along, the line of well-wishers seems to have grown. An hour later, we are down to just a few people in the diner. Matti's curled on his side in a booth, asleep.

"Why don't you go on and take Matti home," I say, as the last person leaves. "I'll stay and help Mom and Gabby clean up."

"No, no," Mom calls from across the dining room. "You two take Matti. I'm sure he'll stay asleep while you drop Lacey off. Right, Knox?"

Knox nods his head. "He's usually out like a light this time of night."

"Good," Mom says, wiping the crumbs off a table. "You two go. I'll help Gabby clean up. There's not too much mess, anyway."

"Are you sure?" I ask Gabby. "I don't mind staying."

She shakes her head. "Absolutely not. This is your engagement night. You don't get to clean up."

"Okay," I say, giving her a quick hug. "Thanks so much."

She nods.

"Tell Ms. Daisy, we really appreciate her letting us use the diner," Knox says. "It worked perfectly."

Gabby grins. "I think she was happier about this engagement than you were, and that's saying something," she says with a chuckle.

Knox blushes and kisses my cheek. "I'm going to get Matti."

"He's a keeper," Gabby says from beside me as we watch Knox walk away.

"Yeah," I say softly. "He really is."

Knox lifts Matti from the booth where he's been asleep for the past half hour or more. "Here we go," he says softly when Matti stirs. "Go back to sleep."

The sight of him being so nurturing does something funny to my insides, making me feel all gooey.

He's mine.

They're mine.

My happily-ever-after.

⬚ ⬚ ⬚ ⬚ ⬚

I hope you enjoyed Bean Wishing for a Latte Love! I'd love it if you would leave a review. Even a star rating helps!

Want to know what happens when Knox, Lacey, and Matti finally make it to Silver Dollar City? Find out in the special Bonus Chapter by joining my newsletter at http://tinyurl.com/BEANBONUS

Aurora meets her match, again, in *You Mocha Me Crazy*. Fall in love with The Coffee Loft: Fall Collection and read about Aurora's funny, enemies to more romance.

If you want more of the Coffee Loft series, you can find the other books here: https://books.bookfunnel.com/thecoffeeloftseries

Ready for Gabby to find her happily-ever-after? Will she give Heath a second chance? Find out in *A Soldier's Wish* today. http://tinyurl.com/SoldiersWish

Want more of the Piney Brook world? Meet Brant and Morgan in *His Christmas Wish* available on Amazon and in Kindle Unlimited. http://tinyurl.com/HCWTiaMarlee

Welcome to the Coffee Loft

a place where romance is always brewing ...

Grab your favorite table over in the corner and be prepared to be swept off your feet. This multi-author collection features some of your favorite sweet romance authors that you already know and love as well as a few new names you'll be rushing to check out.

From cold brews to cappuccinos and frothy frappes, there's something on the menu for every romantic comedy reader. Fake dates, meddling matchmakers, friends-to-lovers and so much more, each stand-alone story is the right blend of sweetness, guaranteed to warm your heart. Happily-ever-after's coming right up!

https://books.bookfunnel.com/thecoffeeloftseries

Also By Tia Marlee

Piney Brook Wishes Series

His Christmas Wish

Sweet Summertime Wishes

Wishing for the Girl Next Door

A Soldier's Wish

Her New Year's Wish

The Piney Brook Wishes Box Set

Standalones in the Piney Brook Wishes World

Sunkissed By My Best Friend

Wishing for Forever

The Coffee Loft Series

Bean Wishing for a Latte Love

You Mocha Me Crazy

A Brewtiful Kind of Love

Coffee Loft Collection

Apple Blossom Ranch Series

His to Adore

His to Have

His to Hold

His to Love

His to Cherish

Hers to Treasure

Sugar and Sirens

Still Yours, Always Mine

Catch Me, If You Can

Sweeter With You

A Little Bit Married

The Last First Kiss

A Little Bit of Christmas

Merry & Bright: The Great Light Fight

Gnome Sweet Home

The Candy Cane Parade

Mistletoe at Midnight

Let's Stay In Touch

You can find me at my website: https://tiamarlee.com
Follow me:
Facebook: https://tinyurl.com/FBTiaMarlee
Instagram: https://tinyurl.com/IGTiaMarlee
Amazon: https://tinyurl.com/AmazonTiaMarlee
BookBub: https://tinyurl.com/BBTiaMarlee
Goodreads: https://tinyurl.com/GRTiaMarlee

Join my reader group: https://tinyurl.com/TiaMarleeReaderGroup

About the Author

TIA MARLEE ENJOYS DELIVERING swoon worthy HEA's in her clean and wholesome romance novels. A small-town girl at heart, Tia's stories have that small-town, Hallmark charm with a dash of real life, and a laugh thrown in for good measure.

Tia is the author of the Piney Book Wishes series featuring unexpected love stories based in small-town Piney Brook, Arkansas. She is also proud to be part of the multi-author romcom series The Coffee Loft season one and two.

Tia resides in Texas with her husband and three teenaged children. When she's not writing or reading, you can find her standing barefoot in her front yard, loving on her 80 pound lap dog, or hauling kids from one activity to the next.

www.ingramcontent.com/pod-product-compliance
Lightning Source LLC
Chambersburg PA
CBHW031606260626
47154CB00020B/1644